HORSE BONES

12 Tales of Secrets, Ghosts and Legends

For Bud – Enjoy!

Ron Miller

Ron Miller

ISBN: 978-1-934666-27-2

Cover Design by Summer Morris

Published and distributed by:
High-Pitched Hum Publishing
321 15th Street North
Jacksonville Beach, Florida 32250

Contact High-Pitched Hum Publishing at
www.highpitchedhum.net

This is a work of fiction. The literary perceptions and insights are based on the author's experience. All names and places not historical, characters and incidents are either products of the author's imagination or are used fictitiously.

To Eric Miller, my sweet blond-haired son who, at sixteen, left for a celestial world where streets are paved with gold; and to his brothers and sisters, Lori, April, Amy, Holly, Adam and Chris, who inspired me to write in the first place.

And to Terri Ridgell, Sandy Callahan, Debbi Kopach, and for a while, Dickie Anderson, my critique partners; and to Tom Silverio, who brought us all together. My love and respect for them are without measure.

And finally, to Jimmy Redmon, who made the ultimate sacrifice for his country.

BOOK REVIEWS

In this fine collection of "tales of the unlikely" Ron Miller spins a web of scary and richly atmospheric stories. Who knew that the piney woods, the boggy wetlands, and the abandoned railroad spurs of north Florida were stalked and haunted by spooks, specters and vibrating balls of light?

With a sure command of character and place Ron Miller will scare and intrigue his readers. His character, Jimmy Redmon, temporary president of the Five Points Spook Club, may cringe as he always says, "I don't like spooky places!" But for those of you who do, *Horse Bones* is a great read.

~Adrian Fogelin, author of *Crossing Jordan*

"I was hooked from page one by Ron Miller's ghosts. I even glanced over my shoulder a time or two to see if there was anything behind me. *Horse Bones* is a must read!"

~Shannon Greenland, award-winning young adult author

"Ron Miller writes with flair and imagination. His *12 Tales* takes us back to a childhood where anything is possible—including a belief in the supernatural. Prepare yourself for a shiver-producing collection filled with strange happening and uneasy pleasures, yet filled with the camaraderie and good humor of its youthful cast of characters. *Horse Bones* is good fun."

~Vic DiGenti, author of *Windrusher and the Trail of Fire*

"If you are over ten years old, you have seen ghosts. They live under the bed or in the shadows of you darkened room. I've seen them and I'm not afraid to admit it. All the way from *Jack-in-the-Box Clown*, who haunts a child's room, to soldiers coming to the rescue, then disappearing, and on to the terrifying Demon Eyes creature that inhabits the dark, dank corners of the swampy woods, these tales will dredge up memories that you had hidden away, or you thought were hidden. Follow the animal trails through the thick underbrush to discover who the real murderer was in Traders Hill. This spellbinding book will keep you up at night, either reading it or afraid to go to asleep."

~David Tuttle, author of *Pirates, Gamblers and Scalawags*

"Ron Miller has put together an amazing collection of spellbinding stories sure to captivate writers and readers alike. Hang on to your hat and let Miller take you for a readable ride."

~Dickie Anderson, Writer, speaker and columnist

FOREWORD

I am deeply honored to be included in this spellbinding collection of eerie short stories. Ron has the amazing ability to use past experiences as springboards to these thrilling tales. His unique talent is to offer you the opportunity to delve within the unknown and unexplained.

Ron and I met over four years ago when six of us decided to form a critique group with the hopes of embarking on exciting careers in writing. Having already established myself as an author, I found it exhilarating to work with the amazing talent of all the members. Soon our group readjusted and we were only five. Another year followed and we found ourselves as a foursome. The core of us knew we had found something special. Ron continued to write additional stories with depth, intensity and realism, as the legends demanded to exist outside of his mind.

So sit back and let yourself be immersed in the many secrets, ghosts and legends—if you dare ….

T.A Ridgell

Terri Ridgell is the award-winning author of *When Opportunity Knocks* and three other best-selling novels.

ACKNOWLEDGMENTS

I would like to acknowledge Paul Massing for his uniquely creative and inspiring art. His illustrations are masterful strokes of genius that tell their own story. I thank Paul for his artistic talent, and most of all for his friendship.

A big thank-you to Janet Cote-Merow, a friend whose advice I value. And to my editor, Beth Mansbridge, who really knows how to put a shine on an author's work.

And to Linda, whose patience, encouragement and unwavering support allowed me to write without guilt.

THE HAUNTING OF LORI MILLER

"I loved the stories my father told me as a child about his unearthly experiences while growing up in Five Points, his North Florida neighborhood. Evidently, I inherited his inclination for things otherworldly. And so did my little brother, Eric."

That's a quote from Lori Miller, the author's daughter. She related the following stories to her father after she was grown. They happened at her grandparents' home during her summer visits.

"Jack-in-the-Box Clown" and "Ghost Soldiers" are tales about the haunting of Lori Miller.

HWY 90
LAKE CITY
LAKE ISABELLA
CEMETARY
EASTSIDE ELEMENTARY SCHOOL
S&S FOOD STORE
S.E. BAYA DRIVE
TRIBBLE ST.
WENDY'S
LAKE HAMBURG
OAKHILL ST.
LORI'S GRAND-PARENTS' HOUSE
S.E. LOFTON GLEN
L.C. COUNTRY CLUB & GOLF COURSE
GHOST SOLDIER
JACK-IN-THE BOX CLOWN
BOAT
CROSSING ROUTE
HWY 441
COUNTRY CLUB RD.
ALLIGATOR LAKE
SLOUGH
N
W
E
S
OLD SEMINOLE VILLAGE
INDIAN BURIAL GROUNDS
WEEPING WOMAN WELL
TO GLOWING HOUSE
HIGHFALLS RD.

JACK-IN-THE-BOX CLOWN

Something had changed about Lori's grandparents' house. She didn't know exactly what that something was, only that there was a disturbing, brooding presence in her bedroom.

The bed, big and comfortable, had always been a refuge from everything grownup, a place for sweet dreams and bedtime stories. Her doting grandparents always made everything safe when they tucked her in at night.

That's the way it had been when Lori was a little girl. But things had changed. Now, the preteen with shoulder-length black hair was afraid once again to go to bed at night—frightened at what lived in the dark.

"Lorrrrrie!" Granny called, silhouetted behind the screen door. "Time to come in and get washed up. Pappy will be home soon."

Lori had visited her grandparents' home in Lake City, Florida, every summer from the time she was a little girl. This favorite place on earth was without a doubt magical.

"Coming, Granny. …Another minute, okay?" Lori, talking with her friend Wendy at the edge of the street, was delaying going inside as long as she could.

"It's just your imagination, that's all," Wendy reasoned. "It's all those stories your dad filled your head with when you were little."

"I considered that too, but that can't be it. I loved those stories. Geez, I was fascinated, not scared."

At the age of five, Lori had sat on the saddle in front of her dad and held on to the saddle horn. Together they rode his bay mare, Queenie, through the forest of scrub oak.

While riding he regaled her with stories about ghost puppies, elves, magic railroad spikes, and other tales of the unlikely.

"Well," Wendy insisted, "I still think you're imagining things."

"No I'm not!" Lori said, shaking her head. "I'm telling you, girl, there's something strange going on in that bedroom."

"Yeah, you!"

"You're *so* a spaz brain." Lori cocked her head and slumped with hands on her hips. "Besides, I'm nearly thirteen. I don't believe in goblins and ghosts anymore."

"Yeah, whatever," Wendy said as she waved. "I've gotta go. See you tomorrow—if you're still alive, that is."

"Like I said, you're *so* a spaz brain. See you tomorrow—early."

Pappy drove up in his old and faded blue Ford pickup. The door creaked as he shoved it open with his left shoulder, and he smiled as he stepped out. His blue shirt carried an official logo that read "United States Post Office."

"Hey, sugar plum," he sang. His kindly face stretched with a beaming smile.

"Hey yourself," she said, grabbing his hand while walking along.

The aroma of southern fare wafted through the screen door. Stepping into the house they were immediately covered with delicious, mixed-up smells of fried chicken, turnip greens and crackling cornbread.

"Helen, I'm home," Pappy called, his melodic voice floating throughout the house. Tired from standing all day at the post office window waiting on customers, he flopped onto the couch to pull off his shoes.

In the meantime Lori headed to the bathroom to wash. Her bedroom door, located at the end of the hallway from the bathroom, stood open. Lori reached for the bathroom's doorknob. She heard something stir in her bedroom. She paused and her senses came alive. Bare feet latched to the tile floor like Gorilla Glue.

She stood there, watching like a hawk stalking prey. *Nothing*, she thought. *Maybe Wendy's right, maybe I am being silly.*

Another flicker. A cocoon of fear wrapped her slender body.

"Oh …" she whimpered.

Lori barged into the bathroom, shoving the door closed with a loud click, and the lock tumbled into place. Quickly she washed and dried her hands. Turning to face the door she reached out for the gold-colored knob. She hesitated. Her heart raced. *What if it's there*?

You're just being silly. There's nothing out there, she argued with herself. *There's something behind that door, I can feel it.* She could sense the closeness. The hairs on her arms bristled; her scalp tingled like pinpricks.

Scream, she rationalized, *that will scare it away.*

No, she argued some more, *you're too old to be acting foolish. Everybody will think you're a big baby.*

Again she reached for the doorknob, but stopped and pulled back. The strange feeling would not go away. Instead, every second it grew stronger and stronger.

Now! The door flew open.

Something stood there and it reached out and caught her arm! She screamed.

"Whoa! It's just me. Didn't mean to scare ya." Uncle Kenny stood in the doorway laughing. "You must be guilty of something, kiddo."

"Yeah," Lori fired back in a shaky voice, "guilty of being your niece!" Embarrassed, she squeezed around him and shot straight for the living room.

Kenny never seemed like an uncle to Lori. He was in the ninth grade and played drums in a rock band. They fought and pestered one another like a brother and sister would.

* * *

The night was warm. Pappy and Uncle Kenny sat in front of the big screen watching the Braves play the Diamondbacks. Granny relaxed in her recliner while reading a book. Talking to Wendy on her cell phone, Lori sat slumped in the corner, her legs hanging over the side of a chair.

"There you go again," said Wendy. "Your imagination's running wild, as usual."

"No it's not, I saw something. I'm not imagining it."

Using her best sarcastic voice, Wendy said, "Okay, tell me what it looked like. Give me every detail, down to the wart on its nose."

Lori could imagine the smirk on her face as Wendy held the phone to her ear. "I don't know, okay? I didn't exactly see anything."

"So," Wendy said, "*who's* the spaz brain?"

"Okay, so don't believe me. You'll be ridden with guilt and tormented for life when I'm carried off in the middle of the night to some secret lair, never to be heard of again."

"Secret lair? See, what did I tell you? It *is* those stories your dad filled your head with."

"You sound like Granny. It's not, honest. I'm scared totally silly to be in that room alone. It's just this weird feeling I have, like I'm not alone, you know, like I'm being watched. It's a bad sorta feeling. I can't explain it."

"You told your grandparents?"

"Come on, Wendy, I'm almost thirteen. Geez, give me a break. They'll think I'm a baby."

"Why, because you sound like one?" Wendy covered her mouth and giggled. "Okay, okay, just kidding."

"Strike two!" the umpire yelled as the ball landed in the outstretched glove of Diamondbacks' catcher, Miguel Montero.

"Come on, Chipper, you can do it," Uncle Kenny cheered. He now stood holding a pretend bat, doing what he could to help Chipper Jones hit the ball.

"Don't you think it's time to say good-night to Wendy?" Granny said, glancing at her granddaughter as she turned the page of her Harlequin romance.

Crack! Chipper's bat met the ball with raw power and sent it over the wall for a home run. Uncle Kenny stood with head cocked, watching the pretend ball sail through the air. His hands were over his left shoulder and his right elbow bent as if he had just taken the home run swing.

Pappy bounced to his feet and pumped his fist. "Yes! Way to go, Braves!"

Lori pushed END on her Razr cell and started to ask if she could sleep with her grandparents. Then she stopped and reminded herself, *I'll be thirteen in three months. They'll think I'm a big baby. Sleep with my grandparents. What was I thinking?*

"What's that you were saying to Wendy about being scared silly? I happened to overhear you."

Granny's question caught Lori off guard. She walked over closer to her grandmother. "Oh, that. Nothing really, we were just talking about ghost stories."

Granny snapped her book closed. "I wish your dad hadn't filled your head with that nonsense at such a young age."

"Oh, Granny, they were just stories, and I liked them, they were fun." Then she asked before realizing it, "Can I sleep on the couch?"

"The couch will likely be tied up until the game is over," Granny said.

A young girl was singing "America the Beautiful" during the seventh-inning stretch. Pappy's chin rested on his chest for an intermission snooze.

A blip of a thought awakened a memory. "Granny, do you remember me saying something about a clown in a box when I was a little girl?"

Granny started to open the Harlequin again, but stopped. "You remember that? You were so young."

"What was it I thought I saw?"

"Aren't you skittish enough without hearing about clowns and such?"

"I'm just curious."

"You were dreaming. We heard you scream. It was awful. I'd never heard a child scream like that before."

"You always said I had a big mouth."

"Sometimes a little *too* big for your own good ... Anyway, you let out this blood-curdling scream. Pappy jumped up and tripped over the coffee table...Did you know that he nearly broke his—"

"Granny!"

"Well, he hopped right up," she said, and cleared her throat, "broken leg and all—he was a lot younger then, you know."

"So, what happened?"

"Well, his leg—"

"No, I mean what happened to me?"

"Patient, dear, be patient. You never could wait, you know."

"Come on, Granny, please."

"Well, Pappy and I ran to your room. You were sitting up in bed staring at the ceiling, screaming at the top of your lungs. When you saw us, you jumped off the bed and ran like a racehorse, wrapped your arms around Pappy's hurt leg—that's as high as you could reach, you know. Well, he picked you up and you kept saying, 'It tried to get me! It tried to get me!' "

"What did I see, Granny?"

"Nothing, sweetie, nothing at all. It was only a bad dream. Sometimes dreams can seem real, you know, especially when you're little. And that's all there was to it, a bad dream."

"Did I say anything, like, what the dream was about?"

"Well, it's been almost eight years and my memory isn't what it used to be. But as I said, you mumbled something about a clown and I think you said it popped out of a box. Isn't that funny?"

The back of Lori's mind held familiar memories, but they only came forward in tiny blips.

Granny's next words nudged her back to the present. "All I know for sure is that you were terrified. It took Pappy quite a while to get you settled down and back to bed. Speaking of bed, I think it's time we both turned in for the night."

"Good idea," Uncle Kenny chided, "maybe then we can hear the ball game."

Granny pulled herself up from the recliner and went to the bedroom. Lori, who had been kneeling beside her, plopped down in her place.

She could feel the comforting warmth of her grandmother in the chair's floral cloth. *This is the way it should be at my grandparents' house, warm and cozy. Nothing bad could possibly happen here.* Reassured, Lori scooted from the recliner and made her way down the hall.

Without warning, darkness fell over her; the safe feeling had vanished. She looked toward the open door of her room.

The Diamondbacks' batter, Jeff Salazar, sliced his bat through the air, connecting with nothing. The umpire did a quick jab with his fist and called, "Stee-rike three, you're out!"

Lori jumped, then shot like a bullet back into the living room, bumping a lamp in the process. She caught it just in time, and then plopped down in the still-warm recliner with the rescued lamp in her hands.

"What's bothering you?" Uncle Kenny asked. "I've noticed you've been awful jumpy lately and prone to destruction of household items."

She had dropped a dish earlier when Uncle Kenny had sneaked up from behind and grabbed her as she cleared the dinner table.

"Nothing. And I'm not jumpy." She placed the lamp back on the end table. "Besides, you're a total doofus."

Uncle Kenny laughed.

"I'm going to bed," Lori announced, hoping to get out of talking about her fears in front of everyone. She flipped on the hall light and shuffled toward her room. At the doorway she stopped, reached in quickly and turned on the bedroom light.

Nothing there except a bed, dresser, nightstand and lamp. In the corner sat a small desk with a Dell computer in "sleep" mode. The parted window curtain revealed soft light from a half-moon. Shrubbery stood in shadows and moved gently with the summer breeze. She rushed over and pulled the curtains closed.

Everything seemed normal, nothing out of place. It was always that way, until everyone was in bed fast asleep. Then things would happen. The mood in the room would become dark and brooding. A chill would settle in and penetrate her bones. Then she would wait.

"Oh," she said, dreading what was sure to come. Time seemed to stop. The windup clock's tick, tick reverberated throughout the room.

So far she had not actually seen anything, only felt it, but she knew *it, something,* was there.

Tick, tick.

"You're out!" the announcer called through the open door.

"Oh no," she whimpered.

The game was over. The announcer gave the score: Braves 3, Diamondbacks 1. The television clicked off and a rustle ensued from the living room...Pappy and Uncle Kenny moving around. Lights were turned off and the two baseball fans took turns in the hall bathroom, the only one in the house.

"Good night, sweetie pie," Pappy said, sticking his head through the doorway. "Sweet dreams."

"Good night, Pappy."

He reached in and turned off the ceiling light, went to his room and softly closed the door.

Lori bounded up and turned the light back on, using the dimmer switch to fade the bulb down to a soft glow. She tumbled back into bed, lay down and pulled the covers to her chin. She waited. Nothing happened. After a while her eyes became heavy with sleep and her head slumped to the side on her pillow.

Someone laughed. Her head jerked forward and her

eyelids popped open. Instantly she felt something evil and menacing in the room with her.

Lori noticed a quick movement out of the corner of her eyes. "Ohhh," she whimpered, and then eked out, "Help."

A whisper of a cold winter wind shook the curtains as something passed. Lori shivered. It laughed again. Not a nice, happy chuckle, but an eerie, evil, taunting cackle.

Terror crawled up Lori's spine. "Help," she sobbed again, her voice hardly audible. She shivered uncontrollably. *Oh,* she thought, *is this it?*

Something appeared over her head, just under the ceiling. The dimmed light now seemed cold and harsh. A square jack-in-the-box floated over her head. It moved slowly, from side to side and began a measured tumble revealing large polka dots on each side. It stopped moving and a muffled laugh came from inside the box: "Hee-hee-hee!"

The polka-dotted box drifted downward. Lori could only stare and wait; her body couldn't move. Her mouth opened wide and she pushed but the scream stayed frozen in her lungs. The thing was bobbling three feet from her face.

"Pop Goes the Weasel" played from inside the box. Wicked cackles accompanied the music.

The crank, protruding from the center of a polka dot, turned without assistance.

Pop goes ...

The lid flew open.

The weasel …

A clown's head dangled from a long, crinkly neck, bobbing up and down. The bright yellow jester's hat flopped back and forth. Another silent scream.

A heinous laugh escaped from a painted mouth that exposed razor-sharp, pointed teeth. A wicked grin crossed its thin, pasty face. The head continued to bobble and the clown's neck stretched closer. Its eyes bulged out as if it were being choked by unseen hands. Lori's heart almost drum-rolled out of her chest.

The clown's neck stretched like an accordion. Its grin widened and eyes glowed like a wild animal in the dark. It kept laughing, "Ha-ha-ha-hee-hee-hee!" Its neck curved downward and mean eyes looked directly into hers. A dark red tongue popped out of its mouth and waggled back and forth.

The laughter increased: "Ha-ha-ha-hee-hee-hee!"

The head lifted up and the crinkly neck recoiled like a Slinky.

That broke Lori's trance. The pent-up screams gushed out like water from a burst dam.

The clown's neck sprang like a striking snake.

She kept screaming. It kept laughing. Then its bulbous red nose touched her nose. Green eyes shined like a cat in the dark.

A silhouette appeared in the doorway. A hand reached through the door. The room became bright. Pappy bounded onto the bed with both knees, grabbed Lori and pulled her close, his cheek resting against her head.

In a voice soft and reassuring, he said, "It's all right, sweetheart, it's only a dream."

Granny stood beside them. "It's those confounded stories again." But Lori knew it wasn't.

* * *

Lori's vacation was over. Her family had just driven up in their SUV. Her sister, April, jumped out of the car and dashed to hug her grandparents. It was her turn to stay. Eric, her little brother, finally managed to unlatch the seatbelt and scooted from the leather seat.

"And that's not all. Lori refused to sleep in her room after that awful dream she had." Granny shook her finger in the face of Lori's dad. "And that's not the half of it. You should stop telling those foolish stories of yours. It's scaring those youngins to death."

* * *

"You should believe me, you know. After all, that's what best friends are for."

Lori stood with Wendy in the front yard saying their goodbyes.

"So, you're sticking to your goofy story about the clown?"

"Totally."

"Do yourself a favor. Go to a circus, paint your face, hire a clown for your birthday party."

"Funny, Warner, you're hilarious."

* * *

Lori's clothes were in Granny and Pappy's room. That's where she had been sleeping on a pallet, not caring if they considered her a baby or not. She even refused to go in the "clown room," as it was now called.

Eric, her five-year-old brother, walked in as Lori was stuffing her clothes into her pink duffle bag.

"Lori," he said, pulling on her shirtsleeve.

"Hey Eric, I really missed you." She smiled and gave him a hug.

"I don't like it in there." Eric pointed in the direction of the "clown room."

"Where, in the bedroom?" A knowing feeling drenched her body.

"Yeah, I don't like it."

Lori knelt so she could look directly into his eyes. "Why?" she asked, already knowing the answer.

"Because it's scary."

"In what way?"

"There's a clown in there, it's in a box and it floats over the bed."

Lori couldn't believe what she was hearing. "What else?"

"The clown has mean eyes and a long neck and its head goes up and down." Eric moved closer and she shuddered. He added, "He laughs crazy and sticks his tongue out, too."

She pulled him to her and squeezed him tight. “Don’t be scared. You just imagined it, that’s all.”

As she spoke, a whisper of cold winter wind stirred the bedroom curtains.

GHOST SOLDIERS

The bedroom lights were off but the room was still bright. The open window let in a summer breeze and the curtains moved ever so slightly. The moon, in its full phase, shined into Lori Miller's room. Shadows hid in the corners where the moonlight could not reach.

From the next room a voice, muffled by walls, rose in pitch, then lowered. Lori knew that her grandfather—she called him Pappy—was probably having those awful dreams about the war again.

The ghostly mist floated like fog in early morning coolness. It drifted, wispy, in and out of view. The vision was not a dream. She was awake.

Pappy mumbled, whined something unintelligible.

The haze brightened. Figures began to form.

Lori scrunched down and pulled the covers up to her nose. The voice behind the wall became animated. More forms in the shape of men emerged from the mist.

Sharp green eyes watched six soldiers stand against the wall, looking directly at her.

"Oh," she whimpered, and pulled the covers up to her wide eyes.

Army soldiers carrying M16 rifles with bayonets stood watching intently, but no longer at her.

Something stirred above Lori's head.

The lead soldier took a step forward, followed by the others.

"Wake up, honey, you're dreaming again."

Granny's voice could be heard from the next room as she shook him gently.

"Leo." Granny shook her husband again. "Wake up."

Pappy woke with a jolt, his breathing ragged and labored.

The soldiers halted and began to fade. The lead soldier reached for something, and then they were gone.

* * *

Four years had passed since Lori saw the jack-in-the-box clown while visiting her grandparents in Lake City, Florida, during summer break. Everyone tried to convince her it had only been a dream resulting from her father's yarns about a glowing house with orbs, a demon-eyed creature or some other mystical being created from an untamed imagination. Nothing else had happened since that night so she had assumed they were right. But now she knew; it wasn't a dream or a product of a child's imagination. There was no doubt. The clown was real and so were the six soldiers standing before her last night.

Lori pushed herself out of bed and stumbled toward the kitchen. School was out and this was the second day of her summer visit. Pappy sat at the table, chair turned slightly, with the *Florida Times-Union* in his hands. He shook it gently to straighten the folds as he turned to page C-3 of the sports section.

Lori, still sleepy, plopped down in the chair beside him and immediately closed her eyes.

"Good morning, sunshine. How was your night?" Granny stood at the stove stirring sausage gravy.

"Okay, I guess."

Pappy lowered his paper and chuckled. "You don't know if you slept well or not?"

"I was dreaming about soldiers until the smell of biscuits woke me."

Pappy had started to raise his paper but stopped. "Did you say soldiers?"

"Yeah, they had rifles with bayonets, muddy uniforms and green helmets." Lori looked at Pappy to watch his reaction. *Is there a connection?*

"Oh, I see." Pappy cleared his throat and scanned the baseball scores.

"One of them had three stripes on his sleeve," Lori told them. "What does that mean, Pappy?"

A puzzled look. "Uh, that's the rank of a sergeant." Pappy rustled the paper and continued reading.

Granny placed a pan of hot biscuits in the middle of the table and sat down. "Your granddaddy's been having dreams, too."

"About the war?" Lori asked.

Pappy said nothing. Although it had been over thirty-five years since he stalked the jungles of Vietnam, the horror of war was still fresh in his mind.

"Yes, about the war … and the sergeant," Granny added.

"Thought so. Heard him talking in his sleep last night." Lori perked up. "Did you say sergeant?"

Pappy remained silent.

Lori picked up a biscuit and bounced it around in her hands before dropping the steamy bread onto her plate. "Got 'ny butter?"

"In the refrigerator," Granny said. "Will you bring it to the table, please?"

Lori retrieved the Land O'Lakes and spread it over the hot bread. "What if I told you I had dreams too, about soldiers, I mean? At least I think it was a dream. It seemed so real, though." Lori took a bite and butter oozed from the corner of her mouth. She knew it was no dream; she just wanted to see Pappy's reaction.

Pappy stopped the fork halfway to his mouth.

"Something wrong, Leo?" Granny reached over and placed her hand on her husband's arm.

"Oh, nothing, just thinking." He lowered the fork back to his plate and reflected for a long moment.

Lori was well aware of her grandfather's service in the war. She was proud of it and prouder of him. He had always been her hero, even before she knew anything about his war service.

Pappy took a sip of Postum. "What are your plans today?" he asked, hoping to change the subject.

"Nothing special, I guess. I'll probably mess around with Wendy, listen to music, you know, stuff like that." Wendy lived down the street, just past the sign that read "Neighborhood Watch."

"After you help me with dishes and a few other chores around the house," Granny reminded her.

"Oh, that too."

After Pappy left for work at the post office, Lori cleared the table and finished her assigned chores.

"I'm going over to Wendy's," she said, pushing the screen door open. "Be back in time for lunch, bye."

* * *

Wendy and Lori sat on the bed with the radio blaring.

"Sweet! This is my favorite song." Wendy reached over and turned up the volume.

Lori turned it down and asked, "Do you believe in ghosts?"

"What? You're so weird."

"It's the company I keep."

"You are so, sooo weird."

"Well, do you?"

"What, believe in ghosts? Maybe, I don't know. I've never seen one." Wendy, sitting Indian-style, hugged her knees. "I suppose you've been seeing clowns again."

"Nooo. Not recently anyway. And regardless of what everyone says, I did see a clown pop out of a box and hover over my head when I was twelve years old."

"I *have* to get new friends."

"I'm the only person that would be seen with you in public. So you're stuck with me."

"That's true." Wendy threw her hands up in mock resignation. "I'll leave town and start over."

"I'll help you pack."

"So, what ghoulish things from the underworld have visited you lately?"

"Ghost soldiers."

"Soldiers? You mean, hup, two, three, four—attention! Yes, sir! That type of soldiers?" Wendy rolled her eyes.

"You're so lame."

Wendy laughed. "Were they good-looking?"

"It's hard to talk to a brain-dead person."

"Well, yeah, tell me about it."

"Geez! Come on, let's walk to the S&S for a Pepsi."

"Walk? Are you serious?" Wendy sounded incredulous.

"Yeah, like, it's only a few blocks away. You won't die. Besides, maybe Johnny Michael's working today. He's totally hot."

Lori and Wendy started for the S&S wearing iPods, one red and one purple. The girls walked along tree-lined streets while music blared in their ears. A squirrel scampered up a huge sycamore, stopping to chatter at the teenaged intruders.

"Ghost soldiers?" Wendy lifted an eyebrow. "Puh-leeze!"

Jasmine wrapped the neighborhood with its sweet aroma. Lori closed her eyes and took a long sniff before responding. "Six of them, and the leader—at least he acted like the leader—was a sergeant. They had guns—"

"Guns? Geez!"

"With bayonets."

"You're serious, aren't you?"

"As a heart attack. I know it's hard to believe…"

"No! Whatever would make you think that?"

"And I know it sounds kooky."

"Yeees, go on."

Lori furrowed her brow. "I don't know why I see these things, but I do. Maybe there's something wrong with me…"

"Well …"

LAKE CITY

"I'm serious, Wendy. I saw that jack-in-the box clown when I was twelve, in that same room, I know I did. It popped out of a polka-dotted box, laughed at me, stretched out its neck and tried to grab me … and I saw the soldiers, too."

Wendy noticed the serious expression on her friend's face.

Lori said, "Maybe you'd like to spend the night and see for yourself?"

"Cool." Wendy kicked a stone and watched it clatter away.

They turned off Oak Hill onto Country Club Road and walked another two blocks to the S&S.

Lori brightened up. She whispered, "There he is."

Johnny was standing at the counter waiting on a customer. He smiled at them when they walked in.

* * *

"Hey, Pappy, sell any stamps?" Lori asked as he stepped out of his battered Ford pickup.

"One or two thousand," he said with a laugh. "Do anything special today?"

"I talked to Johnny at the S&S. He asked me out to the movies this Friday night."

"You're too young."

"I'm sixteen."

"That's what I said, you're too young."

"Please? It's just the movies, Wendy and Rob's gonna go with us, it'll be a double date, so everything will be cool."

"Uh," he grunted. "Well, I suppose it'll be okay if Wendy goes."

"Yeees! Thank you, Pappy." She threw her arms around him and squeezed. "Ummm, I love you."

"But you'll have to be home by eight."

"Pap-py!" She drew back, saw a grin on his face and laughed.

* * *

The evening was warm but pleasant. The pink and white azaleas gave off a sweet scent that wafted through the open living room window on a gentle breeze.

Granny picked up a ball of Red Heart yarn from her knitting box. She said, “I hope you sleep better tonight, Leo.”

“I hope so too.” Pappy stretched and yawned. “It makes for a long day when I don’t get my rest.”

“It keeps me awake too, you know, tossing and turning and talking in your sleep.”

“I know it does. I’m sorry.”

Lori and Wendy were in Lori’s bedroom, ready for bed. Lori had on a pair of pink bunny slippers and a knee-length purple shirt with hearts. Wendy wore a pair of yellow Sponge Bob Square Pants slippers and matching pajamas.

“Sponge Bob?” Lori laughed.

“My favorite. Ghosts are scared of ’im.”

* * *

“You really do need to talk about it,” Granny said, sitting next to Pappy on the couch.

“Now Helen, we’ve talked about this before.”

“Well, you do. You need to talk about it, get it all out of your head.”

“I can’t.” Pappy clicked on the television. A rerun of *I Love Lucy* was on.

“Ay, ya, ya! Luuucy,” Ricky scolded the crazy redhead, “what have you done now?” Soap poured out of the dishwasher, covering up the entire kitchen. Laughter came from the audience.

* * *

Lori and Wendy talked and laughed while listening to their iPods. Granny and Pappy had gone to bed long ago.

“Well, I haven’t seen any ghosts yet.” Wendy looked

around the room. "I've been cheated."

"You've probably frightened them." *Come on*, Lori thought, *prove to her I'm not making you up*.

Lori and Wendy unplugged the electronic Apples from their ears and put them on the nightstand. They lay back on their pillows and pulled the covers up to their chins.

"Good night." Wendy yawned and closed her eyes. "Wake me if any ghosts show up." Within two minutes her breathing became slow and rhythmic.

Lori's eyes grew heavy too but she fought sleep, hoping for something to happen.

A voice in the next room, muffled by walls, rose in pitch, lowered, then rose again. Lori knew Pappy was having dreams about the war again—dreams that haunted him.

A funnel of moonlight streamed through the three- by five-foot window, spotlighting the bed. Corners of the room remained shady with spectral silhouettes of lamps and stuffed animals. Outside, lawn shrubbery danced in the warm breeze while crickets invaded the night stillness, singing in perfect harmony.

Something in the far corner of the room caught Lori's eyes. Alert at once, she sat up in bed. A haze, like rippling water, faded in and out. She tried to focus. Images appeared. They became more distinct. A man, tall and gaunt, turned, arched his shoulders, looked intently at her and stepped forward.

Lori recoiled and pushed back against the headboard. She murmured "Oh" with both hands pressed to her mouth. "Ummmph" squeezed from her tight lips.

Another step forward.

Her feet dug at the sheet, shoving her body even tighter against the headboard.

Wendy, disturbed by Lori's sudden movement, woke from a deep sleep and saw her friend pressed against the headboard, arms spread wide and mouth open. "What the—"

More soldiers materialized.

"Heck is going on." She caught Lori's gaze and followed it. A quick breath. "Uuuh!" Hand to mouth. "Oh my God!"

Splotches of mud soiled the soldiers' uniforms. Grass and vines dangled from helmets in camouflage. The soldiers stared in the direction of the two girls, but not at them.

Wendy pushed up next to Lori and they hugged.

Something stirred above the bed.

"Leo, wake up." Granny's soothing voice floated through the thin wall. "It's okay, honey, it's okay, you're dreaming again."

The ghostly images blinked in and out, in and out, bright to dim and then faded completely from the corner stage. The ancient guardian moon now posed high in the sky, out of view from the open window. Lori's room, dappled with dancing shadows, resembled the stage for puppets on a string manipulated by unseen hands.

* * *

Chirping birds celebrated the coming of morning and aroused the two girls from a self-imposed sleep. JoJo, Granny's Siamese cat, lay on Lori's stomach while purring contently. Barely opening her eyes, Lori smiled at the lanky tan cat with the black face. Lazily, Lori reached over and rubbed his head. He responded in kind by pushing his head against her hand and turning up his purr volume another notch.

"You seem happy this morning." She reached and pulled JoJo to her face, rubbing his soft fur against her cheek.

"Ohhhhhwaah," Wendy yawned aloud, and uncurled from a fetal position, raising her head and looking around. She asked, "Did I dream it?"

"No more than I did." Lori stroked JoJo's long, sleek body, then set him down tenderly on the crumpled sheet beside her. She gazed intently at the corner of the room and the images became clear in her mind—every detail distinct. Six soldiers, she remembered counting as they turned one by one toward her. Their uniforms smudged but proud, camouflaged helmets and rifles donned with bayonets. It was all real. No dream had ever been that vivid. In fact she rarely remembered dreams. *No, it was real,* she told herself.

"Please tell me I was dreaming." Wendy said, sitting up in bed and looking from one side of the room to the other.

"Okay, you were dreaming. Actually, you're a mental case."

"I'm sorry," Wendy said. "I'm sorry I doubted you. I can't believe what I saw last night. I did see it, didn't I?"

"You saw it, all right."

But there was something else, too, Lori thought. *Something the soldiers were looking at—something above my head. But what?*

Wendy seemed to read her mind. "I felt it too," she said.

Granny called from the kitchen, "Lori, Wendy, time to get up."

"Okay, Granny, we're coming."

They yawned lazily and stretched their arms wide in unison. The aroma of frying eggs and Sunbeam toast made their stomachs growl.

* * *

After breakfast they retreated back to the bedroom and latched iPods to their ears. Over the music they talked about the ghost soldiers and what it all meant.

"Seeing the soldiers was spooky," Wendy said, hugging a pillow, "but that other thing in the room …"

"Yeah, it was worse." Lori pulled a pillow to herself, too. "I was scared of the soldiers at first, but now I don't know. The other thing, whatever it was, bothers me more. I think knowing something was there and not seeing it is worse than actually seeing it."

Lori and Wendy scanned the bedroom seemingly on cue. The room featured a soft azure blue paint that radiated comfort and safety. Pictures displaying outdoor scenes and brown-eyed puppies adorned the walls. An oak bookcase with glass doors highlighted Nancy Drew mysteries and fairy tale books on the lower shelf, a world globe on the middle emphasized books on geography on one side and world history on the other. The top shelf held an out-of-date, clothbound set of encyclopedias.

Everything whispered “safe, secure, normal,” but ghosts and *other things* suggested otherwise.

Wendy rolled off the bed. “Whadayasay we forget about ghosts for a while and go get our daily caffeine fix from our friendly neighborhood S&S?”

Lori smiled. “You’re very persuasive. Like, I didn’t know Johnny was made of caffeine.”

“I was talking Pepsi.”

“And a moon pie?”

Wendy laughed. “So, Johnny’s a caffeinated moon pie now?”

“Girl, you’ve gotta get help.” Lori opened the door and gestured. “After you.”

The sun beamed a midmorning high of eighty-five degrees. Kids, on Tuffy bicycles and skateboards with two-headed dragons, whizzed by enjoying their summer vacation.

“Question. Why is it called S&S? Why not Hogley Wogley?”

“You’re sooo weird.” Lori laughed. “But that’s a really cool name for a store.”

A kid on a Flip skateboard zoomed past, wheels making a gravely sound against the pavement.

* * *

“It’s not just the dreams and the remembering that’s so disturbing,” Pappy said, looking haggard as he slumped on the couch. “There’s more to it, something I just can’t put my finger on.”

“I wish you would talk to Dr. Howell.” Granny hesitated, sensing how Pappy would react, but said it anyway: “I’ll make an appointment.”

"No," Pappy said, giving her his determined look.

"But …"

"I don't feel comfortable talking to a quack."

"Dr. Howell's not a duck, Leo, he's a fine doctor, and he can help if you'll only give him a chance."

"Maybe later, after Lori goes home."

She exhaled quickly. "Why wait?"

"Because." He turned to look Granny in the eyes. "Because I don't want to be embarrassed in front of my granddaughter." Pappy clicked the remote and the television came to life.

Lori sauntered in from the bathroom. "So you're embarrassed by your granddaughter *and* you want me to go home?" Her wet hair was bundled up in a towel. "Is that what I heard my loving grandfather say?"

"Of course not," Granny replied, and sat back in her easy chair. "I'm just trying to get your Pappy to see a doctor about his dreams."

"A quack," Pappy added, and then turned up the volume. "She wants me to see a quack."

"Granny wants you to see a duck? No wonder you're embarrassed!"

Pappy and Granny turned to look at Lori, who was smiling. All three burst out laughing.

"The gang will be here in an hour, gotta get ready." Lori pulled the towel from her head, allowing long, black, shoulder-length hair to fall wet and tangled.

"They who?" Granny asked. "Oh, that's right, your date. Remember the rules? No drive-ins."

* * *

"How does Ken's Steak House sound?" Johnny asked. "Rob's paying."

From the back seat of the Dodge Challenger came, "M-m-me? I had to buy your gas."

"Just kidding, cheapskate." Johnny turned up the volume on the CD player.

"Awesome, turn it up some more." Wendy moved to the music. "So, what are we gonna see?"

"A horror movie," Rob said, "at the Lunar Drive-in."

"Horror movie?" Wendy looked incredulous. "That's crazy."

Rob said to Wendy, "Not to worry. If you get scared, I'll be there for you."

A sheepish look crossed Lori's face. "Uh, drive-in?" She somehow had forgotten to mention the "no drive-in rule."

"Yeah," Johnny said, smiling. "Good making-out place."

Lori smiled back. "You can only hope."

* * *

"You go on to bed, I'll wait up for Lori." Granny turned the page of her romantic suspense, *Operation Stiletto*. "You need to try and get some rest."

Pappy stood, paused and then sat back down. "It just occurred to me—I haven't had dreams this intense since Lori's last visit." He swiped his hand from forehead to chin. "They were bad the last time she was here. After she went home, they calmed down again."

"What could her visits conceivably have to do with your dreams?"

"I don't know. But it's like I said, can't put my finger on it." Something else occurred to him. "Don't you think it's peculiar that she dreamed about soldiers?" Without waiting for an answer, Pappy pushed off the couch and ambled down the hall.

Lori's door stood open. He paused. Something moved, light, a shadow … something. An odd sensation stirred within him. He moved closer. A whisper of sound swished past the doorway.

With a click, light filled the room. There it is, Leo assured himself: a bed, a desk, nothing out of place. Pappy turned off the light and went to his room. He climbed into bed and gave a sigh as he stretched out. Edginess lay with him as he fought his way to sleep.

* * *

Granny was reading the last sentence of *Operation Stiletto* when Lori strolled through the door. "There you are." She put down the book and smiled. "Have fun?"

"Awesome."

"I guess that was a yes."

"It was crazy."

Granny looked perplexed. "Now you're confusing me. I'm going to bed."

Lori hugged her. "Good night, Granny, thanks for waiting up."

With the front door locked and lights out, Lori lay fully awake thinking about her date. But her high spirits soon dampened as a mumbling, restless voice filtered through the wall. She realized Pappy was dreaming again.

Static light resembling buzzing electricity, only silent, invaded her room. Images came and went. She sat up in bed. Pappy's voice grew louder. Muffled, unintelligible words penetrated the wall.

Another sound from above. … She jerked up. Springy music came from a box. Lori felt a wave of terror surge through her body. Shuddering, she screamed, violently and prolonged, yet the scream was silent.

A burst of light made the room glow. Soldiers ready for battle stood positioned at the far corner.

A jack-in-the-box hovered over Lori's head. A handle, protruding from the center of a polka dot, turned on its own. The tick of the spring created familiar notes.

All around the mulberry bush,

The monkey chased the weasel.

The soldiers rushed forward.

Silent screams became louder.

The monkey stopped to pull up his sock …

"Hee-hee-hee..." Wicked laughter accompanied the nursery rhyme melody.

Pop! goes the weasel.

The lid popped open.

A soldier with three stripes raised his arm.

Pappy shouted from behind the wall, "Sarge, Sarge!"

The jack-in-the-box clown stretched its neck like an accordion and cackled, "Ha-ha-ha."

The sergeant's arm moved forward.

"Hee-hee-hee."

"Charge!" he commanded.

Lori's lungs pushed frozen screams as the joker drew closer.

"Sarge!" Pappy yelled.

Fabric arms reached for Lori.

Six gaunt soldiers with fire in their eyes rushed toward the bed.

Red cloth hands touched Lori's neck.

The soldiers leapt, grabbed the jack-in-the-box and vanished.

In the next room Pappy lay sleeping. The dreams were gone and a contented smile adorned his face.

THE FIVE POINTS SPOOK CLUB

Five Points is a neighborhood located about two miles north of Lake City, Florida, a small town in the Suwannee River Valley. Keith Dampier, Joe Rea Phillips, Ronnie Miller and Jimmy Redmon grew up there. Together they explored Andrew's Swamp, camped in the woods and fished in Mild Branch, which flowed through their neighborhood. Alligator Lake and the fabled Suwannee River provided them with plenty of channel cat and largemouth bass.

They also had some hair-raising adventures. In the next five stories, "The Railroad Spikes," "The Glowing House," "Demon Eyes," "Ghost Wagon and Horse Bones" and "Weeping Woman Well," certain things really did happen.

Another friend, Randy Hatch, is introduced in "Ghost Wagon and Horse Bones," which took place in the small North Florida town of Branford, a short drive away from Five Points. Keith, Joe Rea, Ronnie, Jimmy, and later Randy, loosely referred to themselves as the Five Points Spook Club.

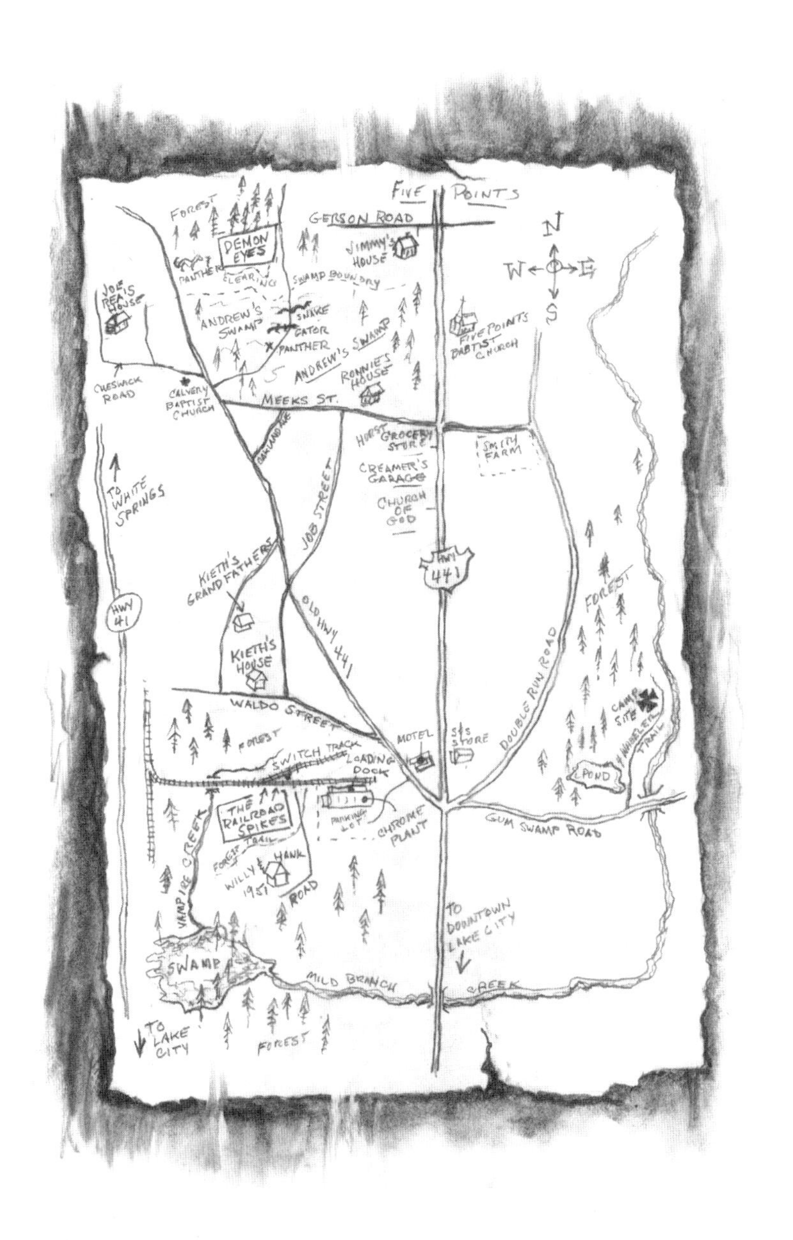

FIVE POINTS
GERSON ROAD
FOREST
DEMON EYES
JIMMY'S HOUSE
N
W
E
S
PANTHER
CLEARING
SWAMP BOUNDRY
JOE REA'S HOUSE
ANDREW'S SWAMP
SNAKE
GATOR
PANTHER
ANDREW'S SWAMP
FIVE POINTS BAPTIST CHURCH
RONNIE'S HOUSE
CRESWICK ROAD
CALVERY BAPTIST CHURCH
MEEKS ST.
HORST GROCERY STORE
SMITH FARM
TO WHITE SPRINGS
CREAMER'S GARAGE
JOB STREET
CHURCH OF GOD
HWY 441
KIETH'S GRAND FATHERS
FOREST
HWY 41
OLD HWY 441
KIETH'S HOUSE
DOUBLE RUN ROAD
WALDO STREET
CAMP SITE
FOREST
SWITCH TRACK
MOTEL
S&S STORE
LOADING DOCK
WHEELER TRAIL
POND
THE RAILROAD SPIKES
PARKING LOT
CHROME PLANT
GUM SWAMP ROAD
FOREST TRAIL
HANK
WILLY
1951
ROAD
VAMPIRE CREEK
TO DOWNTOWN LAKE CITY
SWAMP
MILD BRANCH
CREEK
TO LAKE CITY
FOREST

THE RAILROAD SPIKES

Lake City, Florida – 1951

"Come on, Willy," Hank called, "or I'll leave yo little tail behin'."

"Mama gonna whup us if she know we be goin' to the railroad tracks." Willy rubbed his behind with both hands, remembering what a hickory switch felt like.

"Ah shoot, I ain't no little sissy baby, I be ten years old," Hank said. He stood tall and pushed his chest out. "Sides, Mama ain't gonna find out 'less you snitch."

"I ain't no snitch. But Mama gonna beat us if she do find out."

The brothers ducked behind the backyard chicken coop and then, with bare calloused feet, scampered down a narrow trail leading to the forbidden railroad tracks. Willy and Hank loved trains, especially Willy. They loved the sound of the powerful engine and the feel of trembling earth beneath their feet as the locomotive rumbled by.

"Be careful of rattlers," Hank warned, "they be all in these woods."

"I ain't scared of rattlers, I be scared of Mama's switch."

Ripened blackberries hung heavy on thorny green bushes. Wild grape vines snaked up tall pine trees and gallberry bushes dotted the thick undergrowth. Hank led the way, his brother hot on his heels. Birds fluttered from branch to branch and squirrels skittered up trees as they passed. The brothers trotted along at a steady pace, crunching the carpet of sharp, dry pine needles.

"There it is!" Willy went from a trot to a skip. "Think we'll see a train?"

"Maybe."

"I wanna be a train driver when I grow up." Willy scurried in front of his brother and pedaled backward.

"They ain't gonna let *no* colored boy be *no* train driver! You best get rid of them foolish notions."

A poor black kid could have dreams but little of anything else. That's what Willy had been told all his life. He was young and as yet unfamiliar with the reality of how things were. But right now he saw things differently.

"I gonna be one, jes' wait and see!"

"Ain't neither!"

"Am too!" With that being the final pronouncement Willy pivoted and bounced on the balls of his feet the last few yards to the tracks.

They stood on the tracks waiting. Shortly, to their excitement, a slight tingle ran through their naked feet.

Hank positioned his ear to the rail and listened. His eyes flickered back and forth, a smile gradually widening across his slender face.

"Here it comes," he said, motioning to Willy. "Listen."

Willy quickly placed his ear on the rail. "Sho nuff is!"

"Better get yo tail over here if you don't want to get runned over." Hank tugged on the broken bib strap of Willy's faded Mac overalls, pulling him toward a short section of track used to switch railcars.

"What's that, Hank?" Willy was pointing to the manual rail switch between the spur and switcher tracks.

Hank walked over and examined it. A steel switch box stood on a thick creosote base beside the "Y" formed by the spur and switcher track. A green arrow on top indicated which track the train would travel. The spur track ran directly to the loading docks of the chrome plant. There, chrome produced for the new 1951 Fords was loaded into waiting boxcars.

Hank grabbed the handle and pulled. It moved with a squeak, but not enough. His ninety-pound frame didn't have the strength to completely push the rail over to the other track.

"Come here, Willy, and help me pull this hannle."

"What that hannle do?"

"I don't know, just come do what I tell you."

Hank grabbed the end of the handle and Willy the middle. Both leaned backward as they dug their heels into the dirt and pulled. The spur's rail screeched as it stubbornly moved to line up with the switcher. Now the red arrow atop the switch pointed toward the side track instead of the chrome plant. The brothers, concentrating on pulling the handle, didn't realize the rails had switched directions, changing the course of the train.

The short-nosed GP-9 engine rumbled into view, pulling a string of empty boxcars.

"Ain't it purty?" Hank tugged on his frazzled overall strap with his thumb.

"Maybe the train driver will wave at us when he passes." Willy danced excitedly on top of the crosstie.

The slow, steady rumble from the train's engine grew louder as it approached. Boxcars squeaked and swayed, followed by the ca-chunka, ca-chunka, ca-chunka of steel wheels rolling over the track's expansion joints.

The train approached. The boys balanced on the rails of the switcher. The Seaboard engine surged with a shudder as the conductor applied throttle, giving the heavy locomotive an extra shove. Ca-chunka, ca-chunka, ca-chunka.

"Come on, Hank," Willy shouted over the engine noise, "wave so the train driver will see us. Maybe he'll wave back."

They waved.

The train rumbled, smoke from the diesel engine leaving an acrid smell in the air.

"Look, Hal," the assistant engineer shouted, "there's youngins on the switcher and that's where we're headed."

Reality smacked the engineer full force. Currents of electric fear zapped his body.

The children stood, waving and smiling.

Hal yanked the brake handle. The wheels locked.

The boys waved.

The whistle blew.

The giddy brothers danced about, ebony skin sparkling in the sunlight.

The powerful engine swerved onto the switcher.

"Jump, Willy, jump!"

Willy stood wide eyed, frozen.

"Noooo!" Hal leaned backward until he stood on his heels, both hands wrapped around the brake lever in a death grip. "Stop, durn it, stop!" the engineer shouted.

Hank grabbed at Willy.

Too late.

* * *

Hal and the assistant engineer stood over the two bodies and wept. As if to share in their grief, thunder rumbled and tears fell from a darkened sky.

* * *

Lake City, Florida – 2007

The chrome plant had long been abandoned. Sleek new cars adorned with plastic and fiberglass made heavy chrome a thing of the past. The building now stood empty; a ghost of silent machinery and memories of men sweating for a day's pay were all that remained.

The deserted plant stood west of highway junctions 41 and 441, once the gateway to Florida before interstates were carved out of the landscape in the early sixties. A dilapidated motel with peeling green paint and an ancient neon vacancy sign sat dead and unused in the middle of the intersection.

Five Points was a rural community of mostly small wood-framed houses on treed lots where Keith, Joe Rea, Ronnie and Jimmy lived. Andrew's Swamp stood as the landmark that separated the north neighborhood from the south neighborhood. Joe Rea and Jimmy lived on the north, or Yankee side, while Keith and Jimmy lived on the south, or

Dixie side. That's the way the boys described it. The Dixie side, according to Keith, was the best.

Keith Dampier, athletic, with rock star hair; Joe Rea Phillips, wiry and brainy; Ronnie Miller, beanpole tall and the oldest; and Jimmy Redmon, the generously proportioned and cautious one who shied from anything remotely adventurous. They were close friends, having known each other all their lives. All four boys lived in the shadow of the abandoned plant that once made chrome for the Ford Motor Company.

Keith, Joe Rea and Ronnie stood in early morning coolness at the edge of Andrew's Swamp waiting for Jimmy to arrive. Cypress trees with gray, stringy bark wore tangled mossy beards. Thick vegetation marked the marsh's edge, where they stood each with a foot on his skateboard.

Jimmy, with cane pole slung over his shoulder and a rusty hook dangling from green monofilament line, walked up to the three early comers. "Where's your fishin' poles?" he said, looking from one to the other.

"We didn't bring 'em." Keith flipped open his Sprint phone. "Didn't you get my text message? Thought we'd do something else for a change."

"Like what?" Jimmy put on his cautious look and tapped his foot. "And you know I don't have a cell phone."

"Oh yeah, forgot. We sorta thought it would be fun to follow the railroad tracks behind the chrome plant, you know, see what's there." With his thumb, Keith dragged brown hair away from his eyes.

"Yeah," Ronnie said. "I walked back there once, pretty spooky."

"Cool idea, don't you think, Biggie?" Joe Rea grinned, already knowing his answer. A Blue Tooth stuck to his right ear resembled a June bug attached to tree bark.

"Not me. I ain't walkin' down no railroad track in the middle of the woods," Jimmy said with assurance. "Sides, I don't like the idea of trespassing."

"C'mon, dude," Keith said. "Who are we going to be trespassing against?"

"Rattlesnakes, spiders, redbugs..." Jimmy tapped each finger as he counted. "Yellow flies, bees, skeeters ..."

Keith shrugged his shoulders and drawled, "So, what's the problema?"

"Like I said, rattlesnakes, spiders ..."

"Geez, whatever!" Joe Rea rolled his eyes.

"Besides," Jimmy said, and poked Ronnie on his bony chest, "*he* said that place was spooky back then and I *don't* like spooky places."

"We'll protect you." Ronnie nudged Jimmy in the direction of the chrome plant. "Won't we, guys?"

"Like a Brinks truck," Keith said. "A big Brink's truck!"

Snickers and knee-slapping erupted.

"Shove it, Dampier!" Jimmy said.

A hawk screeched and flew out of the swamp with a snake dangling from its talons.

Jimmy glanced up and shook his head. "Not a good sign, dude, not a good sign at all."

Knowing Jimmy couldn't ride his cane pole, Keith, Joe Rea and Ronnie walked the half mile to the abandoned building with skateboards tucked under their arms.

The teens zigzagged along black tar roads filled with potholes. Ancient wood-framed and newer block houses occupied neat lots with magnolia trees and azaleas. The grassy lot where they played baseball stood empty and alone.

"There is it," Keith said. "Kinda looks dead, don't it?"

Jimmy grimaced at the word "dead."

Across the highway the idle plant stood forlorn and forgotten. Faded red brick walls supported long columns of windows layered with years of grime. Some were broken and others open, having been pushed outward by hands from the past to let out heat generated by machinery and to allow in sunlight.

An abandoned Seaboard Coastline boxcar sat empty at the loading dock, cankered with rust and flaking red paint. The boys stood at the edge of the property and stared at the decomposing structure.

"I'm going home." Jimmy did an about face like a trained soldier. With his fishing pole rifle he started his march.

"Oh no you're not!" Ronnie grabbed his arm and yanked him back.

The track lay on the north side and ran the length of the building for about fifty yards. Immediately past the factory, steel rails emerged from a tunnel of pine trees and thick undergrowth.

"What are we waitin' on?" Keith stepped forward and waved his arm. "Follow me!"

"Creepy," said Jimmy as they skirted the building. "I feel like I'm being looked at."

"You always feel like you're being looked at." Ronnie gave him a gentle shove. "Now, go."

The rusted railcar looked like an ancient tombstone in a derelict graveyard and the building resembled its mausoleum.

Once past the loading dock and boxcar, the four adventurers stepped into the center of the track, lining up single file. With long strides they bounded from one creosote crosstie to the other until they reached the brush line dividing the plant's property from the railroad's right-of-way.

Immediately they were in the woods. To the boys' right lay the switcher track.

"What's that thing?" Jimmy pointed to the switch.

Joe Rea, using his professor's voice, explained, "It's a mechanism that diverts one track to the other."

"Cool, let's see if it works." Ronnie put his board down, grabbed the handle and pulled. The steel rail, frozen in time, moved a tiny bit. "Cool." He let loose of the lever with one hand and motioned to Jimmy. "Come on, Biggie, give me a hand."

Sensitive about his size, Jimmy snapped back, "Move over, you skinny wimp!" He dropped his fishing pole, grasped the handle with both hands and jerked it. The steel rails screeched and moved away from the spur, stopping short of its connection. Jimmy's face turned beet red as he gave a final yank. The rails snapped together with a clang.

Something changed.

Keith, Joe Rea, Jimmy and Ronnie looked at each other, concern etched on their faces. The other skateboards hit the ground. Immediately they grouped together like a school of fish.

"I'm freezing." Keith rubbed his arms. "This is crazy!"

"Dude, what's going on? Geez, I've got chill bumps." Ronnie hugged himself. "Feels like spiders crawling all over me."

Shivering the words out, Joe Rea said, "Obviously a phenomenon of nature."

Jimmy shoved the three aside. "I'm gettin' outta here!" He took off running.

Thwack! And he fell. Air audibly rushed from his lungs with an oooff!

"Yow!" he finally managed to say. Then, with elbows sticking out like short wings and hands next to his chest, Jimmy tried to push himself up.

"Nuts!" he said, and dropped back down.

Keith grabbed one arm and Ronnie the other; together they wrestled him to his feet. Blood dripped from the palms of his hands.

"Ah, geez, look at that!" Jimmy shook the gravel loose and wiped blood onto his white tee.

"Hey! It's warm again," Joe Rea said.

"Crazy," said Ronnie, still holding Jimmy's arm.

"La-go of me!" Jimmy pushed Ronnie's hand away. "I'm leaving. This place is seriously haunted."

Joe Rea gave a weak laugh. "You don't seriously believe that, do you?"

"Yes! Now move outta the way!"

Ronnie grabbed Jimmy's arm.

Joe Rea stepped in front, blocking the way. "There's a perfectly logical explanation for everything," he insisted. "Besides, where's your sense of adventure? How can you call yourself a true Five Points misfit if you run from a little cold air?"

"Cold air?" Jimmy countered. "Think about it. It's late July, genius, in case you haven't noticed."

"He does have a point," Keith said, pushing the hair away from his eyes.

"Think about it, this is really cool," Joe Rea said, glancing around at everyone. "Aren't you the least bit curious as to why we about froze to death back there?"

Jimmy answered, "No!"

"Ah, what the heck," Keith said. "I'm in."

"It *was* awesome." Ronnie looked at Jimmy and said, "Count us in."

Jimmy spit dirt out of his mouth that he had acquired from the fall. His eyes shifted from one friend to the other. Finally admitting defeat, he said, "Nuts! You guys are totally crazy!"

Joe Rea smiled and gave a thumbs-up.

Getting his courage back, Keith said, "Follow me."

The boys started their trek through the woods, cautiously skirting the switch mechanism. Jimmy slogged along yet refused to surrender his spot as number two man behind Keith.

Ronnie, following up the rear, glanced back at the switch. There, where the switch sat, a wispy cloud appeared. Then it was gone.

Ronnie did a double take. "Hey—" He started to say something, then changed his mind.

Yellow pines towered on both sides of the rail bed, leaving it open to the full effects of the midmorning sun. Pungent odors from hot creosote saturated the still air.

"These skeeters are vampires." Jimmy squashed a big

one, leaving a red dime-sized splotch on his arm.

Both sides of the rail bed were lined with deep ditches holding water from a recent rain. A bald cypress swamp, stagnant and foul smelling, lay imposingly off to the boys' left. Out of the swamp flowed a narrow stream with brush-lined banks. A short trestle negotiated the tea-colored water.

Keith, Jimmy, Joe Rea and Ronnie plodded along the gravel-lined rail bed, discussing their eerie encounter. Shadows slid along the ground as they walked.

"It's like a third dimension opened up when we pulled that switch," Ronnie said. "Like *The Twilight Zone* or magic."

Jimmy stopped dead still and spread his arms wide. "Ghost," he said. "That's it!"

"Come on, Redmon, tell me you're kidding." Joe Rea shook his head in disbelief.

Jimmy nodded earnestly. "Durn straight! This railroad is haunted, I'll tell you!"

"Puh-leeze!" Joe Rea said, rolling his eyes.

"Maybe he's right," Keith spoke up. "We've all heard stories about the accident."

"Uh-huh, so you're joining Redmon's Spook Club, too?" A mosquito had bitten Joe Rea on the tip of his nose, drawing a huge welt.

"See? Look at Rudolph." Jimmy pointed at the puffy red nose. "That proves it!"

"Oh, puh-leeze!" Joe Rea rubbed his nose. "It only proves that you Spook Club members have an overactive imagination, that's all."

"Well, we're at the end of the line anyway," Keith said, and turned back toward the way they came.

Stepping past the others he took the lead again, and Jimmy resumed second place.

"Sweet. Now, let's vamoose outta here and go fishin'." Jimmy nudged Keith forward.

Keith took one step. His other leg refused to move. "What the..."

A glint of sunlight bounced off an object lying on the rail.

The boys stared at the piece of steel. No one moved.

Finally Keith stepped forward. "Come on, let's check it out."

The boys, like cats stalking prey, crept within a few feet of the object.

Joe Rea spoke first. "It looks like a spike from the rail bed." He bent down to pick it up.

It moved.

Joe Rea jumped back and yelled, "Holy crap!"

Primed, Jimmy shoved his way through the knot of boys. He stopped, one foot dangling in the air. Immediately he short-stepped backward. "Ah, nuts!"

On the opposite rail lay another spike.

Keith mumbled, "What the heck?"

They matted together like earthworms. As if on cue they looked to their rear. A spike, bent and rusty, drooped across the rail. The boys were fenced in. Deep ditches, briers and high weeds lined both sides of the rail bed, completing the imaginary corral.

"Dude! You see that? How do we get outta here?" Jimmy stood saucer eyed and sweating.

Finally Joe Rea eased toward one of the spikes. "We walk out, that's how." He bent over, picked up the spike and examined it. Then he looked down at the dog-eared fastener covering the outside piece of crosstie. "You see what I see?"

"Yeah," said Keith, looking down, "the hole is empty."

They examined each spot where the spikes sat on the rail.

"Look at this one." Ronnie picked up the bent, rusty spike. "This one has been lying for a while." He examined the dog-ears. "No spikes missing here."

Joe Rea looked around. "Obviously, someone followed us."

"Then how did this thing get behind us?" Ronnie held out the rusty steel he held in his hand. "No way could anybody get this close without us seeing them."

They turned to face the two spikes in front of them. One was gone.

Clink!

They twisted back around.

The missing spike lay on the rail where the rusty spike had been.

Jimmy's saucer-eyed stare moved from the spike on the rail to the one in Ronnie's hand. "Isn't it obvious?" Jimmy's arms became animated. "First the cold air in the middle of summer, then railroad spikes mysteriously appearing out of nowhere—and they move around, for chrissakes. What more proof do you need? This place is haunted, I'll tell you!"

Ronnie looked at Keith, then at Joe Rea, and finally at Jimmy. "Duurn," he drawled. He loosened his grip on the spike, letting it clatter to the ground.

They ran.

"Wait for me," Jimmy shouted. His head bent forward like a sprinter but his legs moved like cold syrup. His breathing became ragged as he stumbled along. Finally he stopped, out of breath, dropped to his knees and rested both hands on the warm crosstie.

Keith looked back, saw Jimmy and then staggered to a stop. Feeling ashamed, he shouted, "Hey, you guys wait up!" He forced out the command between gulps of air. "Let's wait up for Jimmy."

They stopped.

"Bummer," said Joe Rea softly, feeling a little embarrassed.

"Come on," Ronnie said meekly. "Let's go back and help the big guy."

Keith, Joe Rea and Ronnie trotted back and sheepishly helped Jimmy to his feet.

"Uh, sorry 'bout that," said Keith. "I guess we got a little spooked back there."

"That's cool, don't worry about it." Jimmy smiled and said, "Hey, Joe Rea, welcome to the Spook Club."

The newly organized Spook Club stepped from one creosote tie to another. With a heightened sense of caution they remained vigilant for any signs of danger. The switcher track came into view. The memory of the frigid air flooded back. As one, they shivered.

"Oh my God, look!" Jimmy pointed to a grainy mist surrounding the switch.

The boys froze on the spot. Between the two tracks two grainy figures moved. The indistinct boy-sized figures became animated and seemed to be bantering with each other.

The specters stopped what they were doing, turned and faced the boys. They began to wave excitedly as they danced about.

Then they were gone.

"Ghosts!" Jimmy said.

The boys, pale from seeing the vision, decided to find another way around the switcher. Water-laden ditches on either side of the tracks prevented their escape through the woods. Going back was not an option. They had no choice but to continue forward. Cautiously the teenagers moved east toward the switcher.

A series of spikes lay on the north rail, where it veered onto the switcher. There, directly across from the switch, sat two spikes close together, both pointing in the direction of the switch. The switching mechanism, reddish brown from years of rust and supported by a cracked creosote base, held a faded red arrow pointing in the direction of the switcher.

"Here we go again." Jimmy's voice held dread and so did his face. Perspiration beaded his already hot forehead and channeled down his face, where it dripped from his chin. He whispered, "Nuts."

The boys stepped into the cold; winter immediately chased July to another place.

Jimmy made himself the hub and his friends the spokes. Together they shivered past the haunted switcher.

A noticeable rumble pierced the stillness. Starlings clustered in nearby trees sprang from limbs and whooshed through the air. The steel tracks vibrated softly, like a tremor from a distant earthquake.

The human hub and spokes came to attention.

In a restrained voice, Keith said, "Come on, let's go."

They moved as one, setting their sights on the derelict boxcar ahead. Keith, Joe Rea and Ronnie wanted to run, but didn't. Instead they moved at a slow trot so Jimmy could keep up.

Jimmy's chest heaved. He mumbled, "Wait up, I've gotta rest." Gasping, he leaned against the abandoned boxcar parked at the old loading dock.

Keith, Joe Rea and Ronnie, also exhausted, stopped to rest.

"Dude, am I glad to be outta there," Keith said.

"You got that right!" Ronnie gave a thumbs-up and Joe Rea shook his head in agreement.

Then Jimmy noticed something wasn't right. A feeling of danger flooded his brain.

His friends noticed too.

Jimmy pulled back from the car, which had transferred a streak of powdery red paint onto his shirt.

The boxcar suddenly swayed on its axles.

The boys crabbed backward, fell and sprawled over each other.

A heavy groan escaped from the innards of the rusty car.

The boys became immobile as fear plodded up their spines.

A moaning screech cut the air—steel rubbing against steel.

"Aaaaah!" They yelled in harmony and scrambled to their feet. Sneakers bit into the earth and legs pumped, sending sand and gravel flying. Jimmy fell behind. Ronnie and Joe

Rea turned, grabbed him by his arms and yanked. Jimmy's head snapped back as he was snatched forward.

"Come on Biggie," Joe Rea prodded, "you can make it."

Keith, wanting to help, placed both hands on Jimmy's back. Together they pushed and pulled Jimmy along until they reached the highway. Sneakers slapped the pavement as they hurriedly crossed to the other side.

Once safe on the far side, the boys stopped to catch their breath.

"What just happened back there?" Keith asked, pulling up his tee shirt to wipe his forehead.

"Yeah," Joe Rea chimed in, "what in the heck *was* that?"

"Ghost, that's what," said Jimmy with a matter-of-fact look.

They gazed across the highway at the rust-burdened boxcar, glad to be out of its reach.

Then Joe Rea exclaimed, "Durn! We forgot our skateboards!"

Jimmy straightened his arm and gave the stop command. "No way am I going back there! It … whatever, can have my fishin' pole, I'll cut another one."

* * *

Jimmy lay in the semi-dark room staring at the popcorn ceiling. Thousands of plaster bumps resembling a star-filled sky in a vast universe stared back. He pondered over the day's events and wondered if everything had been imagined. Had they been four adventurous friends ready to see and believe anything, or did it really happen?

No, he confirmed in his mind, *it was real!* He had felt the arctic air seep through his bones like wet snow. He remembered the skiing trip to Snowshoe, West Virginia, last winter and the cold air at the tracks had reminded him of that. He shivered. With both hands he pulled the sheet over his shoulders. He sank into the mattress and let the foam shape to his body.

I was there. I saw the spikes, felt the cold air. Jimmy knocked all doubt out of his mind as he stretched the sheet to meet his chin.

He recalled something else. *Funny, how I never felt threatened by the spikes.* He locked his hands behind his head and thought it over. The way the spikes moved from place to place had seemed almost playful. *But the cold air was different*, he contemplated. That had seemed more like a warning. He shook his head, agreeing with his thoughts. Then he wondered, *Why was it cold at the side track and nowhere else?*

Jimmy thought about the gruesome stories he had heard about the two boys killed by the train. A rippling chill tumbled through his body, prompting Jimmy to pull the covers tight around his neck. The story wasn't a new one; he had heard it since he was a kid. But, like other kids, he had thought it a tall tale to frighten them from playing on the railroad.

"James, don't go near the railroad," he could hear his mother say.

A thought totally out of character popped into his head. *I need to go back.*

That scared him. He sat up in bed. "You've lost it, Redmon," he verbalized. "But don't worry, big boy, your brain briefly went south, a freak of nature, temporary insanity, so get over it. You didn't mean it, brain. Did you?"

Yes!

"I was afraid of that. So, ten in the morning, okay?"

A voice in his head said, *Leave early, you'll need to be there by ten.*

"You're very insistent, brain. And, I might add, permanently insane."

Thank you.

"Don't mention it."

Somehow he had always known that he'd go back. The one thing he didn't understand was why.

Jimmy reached over and pushed the SET button on the red-faced LCD clock and then punched in a nine, making sure the AM light was lit up.

* * *

"I know what's wrong with you, Keith, old boy, you've lost your mind," Keith mumbled to himself as he slipped into a pair of Wranglers and threw on a faded AC/DC tee shirt. "That's it! There's no other explanation for getting up at eight thirty on a perfectly good Saturday morning." He shoved into black Nike kickers and headed for the door, grabbing his cell off the oak dresser as he passed.

Once outside he stood and gazed at the overcast sky. The low, gray clouds reached from horizon to horizon, completely blocking the sun from view. Not knowing why, except that he felt compelled, he started walking toward the chrome plant.

Beep, beep! Keith pushed the release on his cell holder and looked at the phone's window: *ru there, KD RM?* The text was from Joe Rea.

Keith replied, *yaak,* for *yes, alive and kicking.*

Ronnie was next to respond with *sh (same here).*

"So," Keith muttered, "they're as insane as I am." With both thumbs he typed, *cu at swamp road.*

Joe Rea confirmed with *npcya*, which is short for *no problem, see ya.*

K, Ronnie agreed, *cya.*

A few minutes later, Keith, Joe Rea and Ronnie stood at the edge of Andrew's Swamp. A slow rumble crawled through thick layers of clouds.

"I had this overpowering feeling that I should go to the tracks behind the chrome plant," Keith explained. "Just don't ask me why."

"Same here," Ronnie agreed.

"That's a ditto for me," said Joe Rea.

"Hey," Ronnie asked, "what about Jimmy?"

"Jimmy?" Joe Rea laughed and said, "Why, he's scared of his own shadow. No way would he go back there again, especially alone."

Keith spoke in a low voice. "I have a feeling he's already there."

The boys looked at each other. "Geez," Ronnie said. "Come on, let's go."

Thunder grumbled like an old man as the three made their way down the road toward the chrome plant.

The sky darkened; black clouds billowed and swirled, further diminishing the sun's dusky light.

The Spook Club, minus one member, walked through the neighborhood, observing its residents.

Mr. Andrews walked behind his ancient Snapper mower, trying to beat the rain. Old Joe Patterson, the neighborhood drunk, staggered his way home from a night at Lawrence's Bar.

Mrs. Rowe, wearing a faded housedress with sunflowers, sat on the porch drinking coffee. "Good morning, boys," she sang.

"Good morning, Mrs. Rowe," the teens chimed together.

"Better get inside," she warned. "Looks like rain."

"Yes ma'am, we will," they assured her.

Then they were there. Under darkness of a worrying sky the old plant sat there, somber, as if in mourning, brooding over lost glory of men and machines that once gave it purpose. Now it sat silent, empty and forgotten, with no purpose except to decompose, crumble and fall.

* * *

Jimmy's heart pounded like a sledgehammer against steel. His legs barely held him up as he approached the rusting boxcar. *It's watching me,* Jimmy thought. He imagined eyes hidden in the corroded steel walls of the railcar … following his every step. Then, when he was close enough, it would sway and yawl like a ship on rough seas. Wrinkled hands would jut out, grab him by his head and yank, pulling him inside its decaying belly.

He shook with fright and clasped his hands over trembling knees to steady them.

"Nuts," he whispered. "What are you trying to prove, Redmon?"

He answered himself. "That you're not a coward, that's what!" That's not why he was there, not entirely, but he couldn't know that. He did know, without doubt or explanation, something was pulling him like metal to a magnet.

He passed the boxcar and loading dock. His measured walk turned unsteady when he negotiated the crossties connecting the rails.

The property line ended. Ahead, a column of trees bordered each side of the railroad track, making it appear like a tunnel through the woods. The switcher track veered off like a wayward child. The ancient switch sat inattentive at the edge.

Go! He urged himself forward with a single step.

So far, so good. He took another step, then another. Soon he was directly across from the track switch. A snake coiled, ready to strike—that's what it felt like. Jimmy kept his eyes focused, his brain alert as he walked slow and steady.

A tinkling metal-against-metal sound…he glanced down. A railroad spike rested across the rail.

"Nuts!" He jumped, and pedaling backward, the heels of his shoes caught the opposite rail, causing him to spill over with a whump.

"Durn! Double durn!" Sprawled like a snow angel, his arms rested in the brush while his legs pointed upward where they rested on a bed of gravel.

Jimmy rolled onto his stomach, and placing both hands on the ground, heaved himself up.

Two spikes now lay side by side, their ends pointing toward the switch.

"Ah, nuts!" His heart shifted into sprint speed: thumpta-thumpta-thumpta. His chest heaved: thumpta-thumpta-thumpta.

Jimmy stood between the two tracks. The arrow atop the switch, red on one side, green on the other, pointed toward the spur where he had moved it the day before. The arrow glared an ominous red!

Thumpta-thumpta-thumpta. His heart was a racehorse stretching for the finish line. Thumpta-thumpta-thumpta.

Solid ground gave way to a sea of vibrations. A train whistle reverberated down the forest tunnel. Jimmy wanted to run but couldn't. His legs, already weak, turned to Jell-O. He dropped to his knees and leaned against the switch housing for support.

"Oh, durn! Oh, durn!" He closed his eyes and hunched his shoulders as if preparing to be hit. The wind picked up, dark clouds churned to the thundering of his runaway heart.

Jimmy felt something else … a presence. His eyes opened like a window shade. Two fuzzy images with outstretched arms held on to the lever of the switch box.

Jimmy whimpered while crabbing backward, his sneakers kicking up dirt.

The two images leaned forward, digging in with the balls of their bare feet, pushing, straining. A child's voice pleaded. The handle moved but not enough to divert the track. The already cold air changed to arctic freeze.

A locomotive rumbled into view. The Seaboard engine shuddered as it throttled up to give the trailing cars an extra pull.

Steel wheels gyrated over the tracks: click, ca-chunk, click, ca-chunk.

The two images moved over to the side track and stood on the rail. They seemed to be jumping and waving. Their lips moved but the engine drowned out the words.

The big GP-9 approached. The engineer shouted something, waving his arms in frenzy. The whistle screamed.

Jimmy lay on the island, propped up on elbows and gripped in absolute fear. His hands clawed the dirt.

Three more images appeared on the track, mingling with the two already there.

The engine's wheels locked. Metal grabbed for metal.

In a flash Jimmy recognized the three images: Keith, Joe Rea and Ronnie.

The locomotive screamed onto the switcher. Jimmy's friends stood in the middle of the track.

The whistle shouted.

The boys stood motionless.

Adrenaline pumping, Jimmy leapt to his feet and dove like a linebacker.

The rumbling monster groaned and screeched.

The four boys plummeted to the side of the track.

The train lurched to a stop. Boxcar couplings clanged, echoing through the tunnel.

It began to rain.

Jimmy, Keith, Joe Rea and Ronnie lay still for a long time, too afraid to move.

The rain fell cool and refreshing, the air a July summer warm.

Standing by the track switch, two boys who loved trains danced about in bare feet, unseen by the four friends. Their smiles turned to carefree laughter as they faded to another world.

Then, slowly, cautiously, the teenagers tugged each other from the gravel bed. They looked around wide-eyed and shaky. The track was empty.

His voice quivering, Keith said, "That really creeped me out, dude."

Together they walked over to the abandoned skateboards, flipped them up with the toes of their sneakers and tucked them under their arms.

"Here's your pole," said Ronnie, handing it to Jimmy. Slapping him on the back, he crowed, "You the man!"

The three boys surrounded Jimmy, rewarding him with an abundance of back slaps, high-fives and “You the man!”

The rain drizzled to a stop. A warm sun peeked out from parting clouds, shooting slanting rays of light toward earth.

“Let’s go fishin’.” Jimmy slung the cane pole over his shoulder and stepped forward. Keith, Joe Rea and Ronnie followed.

A train whistle sounded in the distance.

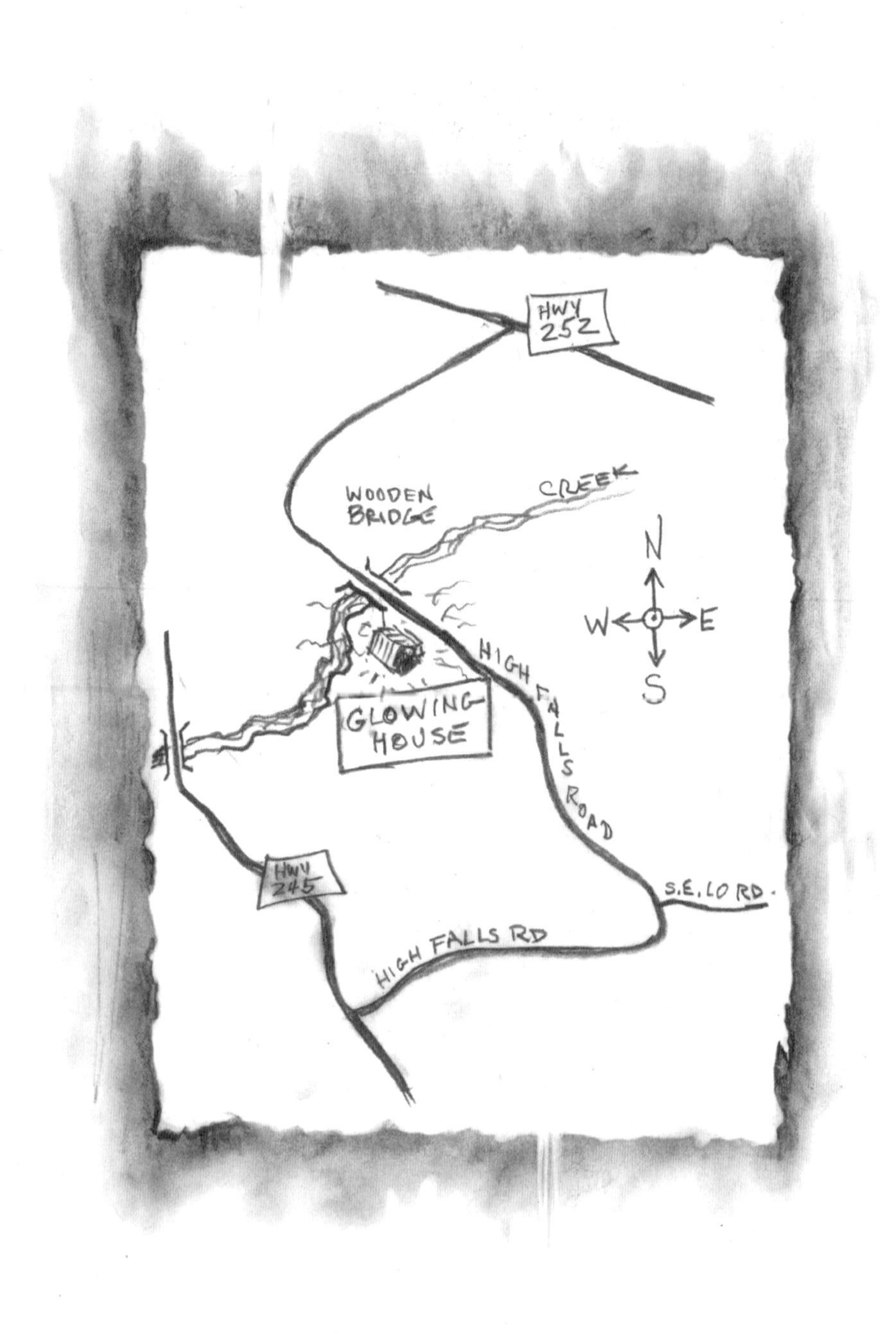
HWY 252
WOODEN BRIDGE
CREEK
N
W
E
S
HIGH FALLS ROAD
GLOWING HOUSE
HWY 245
S.E. LO RD.
HIGH FALLS RD

THE GLOWING HOUSE

Keith, Joe Rea, Ronnie and Jimmy sat parked on their Honda FourTrax Recons with engines running. Every few seconds one would give a twist of the throttle followed by a rapid burst of the four-stroke engine. They were anxious to ride but had nowhere in particular to go.

All four teens wore identical helmets, red to match their four-wheelers. Keith pulled his off and dropped it to his side, gripping it in his right hand. He turned the key to *OFF*, killing the engine. So did the others.

"Have an idea." Keith leaned forward, flashing an infectious smile, rock-star hair fluttering in the breeze. "I heard about this old house way back in the boonies off of County Road 245."

Jimmy flinched.

"Bobby told me about it," Keith continued. "Said it lit up, sorta glowed, like a halo." Bobby, a senior at Lake City's Columbia High School, lived next door to Keith.

Instantly, the bizarre railroad spike incident of a year earlier flashed through Jimmy's mind. He didn't want to hear another word.

Joe Rea and Ronnie leaned into Keith, eager for more.

Jimmy's considerable stomach knotted up. He couldn't fathom his friends' enthusiasm about the unexplained and otherworldly.

"And how did Bobby find out about this haunted house?" Joe Rea asked with delight. Slender and brainy and a masterful musician, his mind appreciated the wonders of man and nature. His soft brown eyes sparkled. A year earlier he had been skeptical, but his encounter with a phantom train had made him a true believer.

"Bobby heard about it from one of his buddies. He talked his girlfriend into going with him to check it out last Saturday night. So, they drove up to the house and parked just inside the yard."

"Parked?" Ronnie snickered. "Sounded like an excuse to me."

"Yeah, sounds like something we would do," Jimmy said, perking up.

"Dude," Joe Rea chided, "you wouldn't know what to do if you *did* park with a girl."

Snickers erupted.

Jimmy shot back, "Yeah, like *you* would!"

"What about this glowing house?" Ronnie asked.

"As I was saying before Biggie went into fantasy land," Keith continued, looking from one to the other, "Bobby and his girl parked and cut the lights off."

"Like I said, sounds suspicious," Ronnie said.

More snickers.

"Hey, Miller," Keith said, dropping his arm to his side, "you gonna let me finish or not?"

"Okay, okay, finish already … geez!"

As soon as the car lights went off, the outside of the house lit up, like a halo. Scared the pee out of 'im. The girl started screaming…freaked her out big time."

"You're trying to wig me out, right?" Jimmy shifted on his seat.

"Wigged out? Because Bobby parked with a girl or because he saw a halo around the house," Keith scoffed.

"Shove it!" Jimmy did an upward motion with his arm. "Okay already, so what happened then?"

"He said this old-timey music started playing…from the house…and when it did, something weird started to happen in the wood surrounding the place. Giant fireflies—or at least something resembling giant fireflies—appeared everywhere."

Joe Rea laughed, saying, "Be real. That sounds more like a bad science fiction movie than a haunted house. Okay, so what happened then?"

"Like I said, the girl was freakin' out, so he had to leave," Keith said. "So, whaddya say, the Spook Club gonna check it out?"

Jimmy's stomach fluttered.

"Sounds sweet," Joe Rea cheerfully agreed. "I'm in."

"Yeah, sweet," Ronnie decided for Jimmy. "Count us in too."

Jimmy groaned, shrugging his shoulders in resignation.

"Tell your folks you'll be staying at my house tonight," Joe Rea suggested.

Hands filled with cell phones, Jimmy waiting to use Ronnie's.

"And you'll be crashing at my house," Keith said, giving Joe Rea a ready excuse.

Keith, Joe Rea, Jimmy and Ronnie tugged on their helmets, and with a press of the ignitions, the powerful engines burst into life.

"Follow me," Keith commanded, taking the lead.

The Recons accelerated down a two-lane country road toward the abandoned house.

"Yee-hi," Joe Rea shouted, "the Spook Club rides again."

The peaceful countryside resembled a landscape painting, with sturdy white farmhouses and gray leaning barns. Crops of corn, tobacco, watermelons and hay waited in crowded fields to be harvested.

Horse-tail clouds wisped across sky red from a waning sun. Cows lowing in green pastures prepared for night and a roan horse standing with his head over barbed-wire fence backed up and whinnied as the four-wheelers zoomed past.

Keith eased off the throttle, slowing to a gradual stop. The Recons behind him geared down, decelerating the engines to idle.

"That way," Keith instructed, pointing east. "Follow my lead." With a twist of the throttles they were off again in search of adventure.

"I have a bad feeling about this," Jimmy mumbled to himself.

Knobby tires sang over rough pavement as the boys traveled the mile distance to High Falls Road, where they turned south. The narrow washboard road, not graded since last week's rain, made their ride bouncy and rough. Runnels spider-webbed across packed sand downward toward shallow ditches, the rainwater long gone. Dusk-gray turned to a moonless black. The lights on the four-wheelers bobbed up and down as the ATVs wheeled over rippling sand waves.

After about a half mile of rough travel Keith applied the brake, igniting the red taillight. The motorcade squeaked to a halt.

"There's the Rose Creek Bridge Bobby mentioned," said Keith, motioning. "The old house is supposed to be on the other side, just past that bend in the road."

A narrow wooden bridge with steel cattle gaps on either side suspended over a shallow creek that flowed from west to east. They crossed single file. The ATVs ka-plunk-ka-plunk-ka-plunked over wide-gapped planks.

Things happened right away.

A light filtered through dense trees and tall brush. The faint glow throbbed: bright, dim, bright, dim, like a heartbeat growing brighter with each beat.

Jimmy shoved the brake pedal, bringing the Honda to an abrupt stop. "Do you see that? That's it, I'm turning back!" He punched the Recon into reverse. His headlight dimmed.

Then all four headlights faded to a weak yellow. The engines lost power. The boys twisted the throttles. Wa-waa-waaaaa …. Each engine died with a lurch.

"What the heck?" Joe Rea's voice drifted from a black void.

Only the silhouettes of ATVs and riders were visible.

"I knew it! I knew it!" Jimmy pressed the starter. Reeeeeclick-click-click. Nothing. "Nuts!"

Then it was gone.

"It's stopped." Ronnie stepped off the Recon. Taking off his helmet, he placed it on the middle of the seat and said, "That was crazy!"

Then the boys noticed something else.

"Oh, crap!" Jimmy shoved his plump thumb against the starter button. Nothing!

Faint globes of light dotted the forest. Dozens floated about like bubbles from a giant wand. Some were small points of brightness, like dust in streaked sunlight. Pale and transparent, others varied in size.

"Orbs," Joe Rea whispered. "They're orbs."

"Will they hurt us?" Jimmy asked, his voice brimming with panic.

"I don't think so."

Everyone huddled around Joe Rea.

"From what I've read, scientists think they're caused by some sort of electromagnetic interference." They huddled closer, and he added, "Some of the paranormal goofballs think they're ghosts waiting to pass over to the other side."

Glaring at the dancing lights, Keith asked, "What does that have to do with our four-wheelers wimping out?"

"They feed off of energy," Joe Rea explained. "They've zapped all the power from the batteries."

"Oh, crap! Look at that!" Jimmy vise-gripped Ronnie's arm.

"Ouch! Let go, lard butt!" Ronnie cried, prying Jimmy's hand loose.

Orbs of splattered light changed from one shape to another.

"Look at that!" Keith peered out from the worm knot they had formed. "What are those shafts of light going from one orb to the other?"

"Energy lines," Joe Rea explained. "They're called energy lines. They feed off one another."

Jimmy asked in a shaky voice, "Do they feed off people?"

"Dude, look! You see that?" Ronnie hunkered down and hugged himself. "Faces, dude, they have faces!"

A basketball-sized orb hovered nearby. It moved closer. The worm knot backed up. The orb followed. Its brightness increased. The knot moved faster.

"Look at that! Look at that!" Jimmy started to hyperventilate.

A somber face appeared inside the globe.

The haunted ball shifted over the boys' heads.

Jimmy dropped to his knees.

The orb dipped closer.

Other orbs joined the basketball. Soon they had completely surrounded the frightened teens.

"We're gonna die, we're gonna die!" Jimmy rocked back and forth on his knees, his hands covering his eyes.

"Oh my God, they're getting closer," Keith yelled. "They're all around us!"

Suddenly, music began to play.

The orbs backed off.

Scratchy phonograph music floated through the humid night air.

Like winking fireflies the orbs blinked out one by one.

The darkness was total again.

Pointing in the direction of the house, Keith whispered, "It's coming from over there."

Jimmy was still on his knees, the toes of his sneakers buried in dirt.

"Come on, get up," Ronnie said, prodding him.

Jimmy didn't budge. His elbows rested firmly on his knees, stocky arms wrapping his head like a shield.

With a good deal of effort Ronnie managed to tug them free. "Quit calling your mommy and get up, for crissakes."

"Hey, Macho Man," Joe Rea said, giving Keith a shove. "What happened to you?"

"I wimped out."

Jimmy struggled to his feet. "Oh, great," he said in a

voice resembling a bleating lamb. "If you wimped out, we're all in deep dukey!"

* * *

Roaring twenties music, tinny and scratchy, seeped through the night. Immediately the stranded teenagers formed TV images of women in flapper dresses twirling beads and dancing the Charleston in a forbidden speakeasy. They imagined men in dapper gangsta rapper suits drinking prohibition whisky and throwing dice.

Keith, Joe Rea, Jimmy and Ronnie, busy contemplating their next move, were startled by a halo of light emerging over the forest canopy. The stark darkness surrounding it resembled a candle in a cave.

Keith, suddenly defiant, hitched up his Wranglers. "Come on, let's go see what all this bull crap's about!"

Joe Rea perked up, "Sweet! Macho Man's back."

"Nuh-uh!" Jimmy crossed his arms, equally defiant. "I ain't goin'!"

"Okay then." Keith was resolute. "Stay by yourself. Come on, men, let's go."

Like soldiers marching off to war, Joe Rea and Ronnie fell in beside General Keith. The speakeasy music continued to play.

Jimmy dropped his arms in resignation. "Wait up," he said, squeezing into the middle of the conquering army.

"Didja bring your mommy?" Keith taunted.

"Shut up, wise butt," Jimmy shot back. "You didn't exactly act like Rambo back there. Besides, I'm not scared, just a little nervous, that's all."

* * *

Rose Creek ran silently past the low wooden bridge, meandering unobstructed through the forest. The sounds of the night were drowned out by loud, boisterous music from the glowing house.

The determined army marched unhurriedly over the uneven road, careful not to fall into a pothole gouged out by recent rains. They were in the woods, alone, they realized, without a way out except to walk. Bravery seemed the only option at the time.

Keith, Joe Rea, Jimmy and Ronnie rounded the bend into the full effect of the pallid light.

"Probably the moon," Ronnie said.

"What moon?" Joe Rea planted a clammy hand under Ronnie's chin and nudged it skyward. "Do you see a moon, lame-o?"

"Darn!"

The music stopped. The four ghost hunters stepped into the now pulsating light. It dimmed to a soft glow. The strobing stopped. The house itself sat imprisoned amidst the circle of light, its windows darkened.

"Ah, nuts," Jimmy whispered. Without realizing it Jimmy had clutched Ronnie's and Joe Rea's arms in a death grip. Neither had noticed.

The aura, completely engulfing the house, extended to the tree line and formed a novelty-shop globe. A perfectly raked, sand-covered yard glistened in the pale light.

Ronnie asked, "Why does the yard have sand instead of grass?"

"That's the way they used to do it in the old days," Joe Rea said. "It was easier to maintain than grass. They just swept it with a rake."

The four boys took in the strange scene, spellbound. The orbs were back.

Jimmy noticed them first. "Nuts!" he said and squeezed even tighter.

"Ouch! Leggo," Joe Rea hissed, prying his arm free.

"You can let go of me, too." Keith wrapped his hand around Jimmy's other hand and pried. "Just chill, dude. It's cool."

Jimmy eased his grip.

"The light," Joe Rea concluded, "seems to energize the orbs, like our batteries did. … But, not to worry. They can't hurt us. I think they're only curious." This seemed to pacify their fears because Joe Rea the Brain had said it.

The house was clearly old. Gray oak boards, cracked rough and faded, had been liberated of paint decades earlier. Intricately scrolled columns supporting the roof were once works of art, but now stood in a state of decay. Rotted steps led to a porch sagging with memories of a past life. And something else.

"Wow, this is crazy," Ronnie whispered. "What's going on here?"

Keith shrugged his shoulders, saying, "I don't know, but somebody should check it out."

Ronnie stared at Keith. "Somebody, as in one of us and not you?"

"Macho Man's getting wimpy again," Joe Rea said, and smirked. "Just like someone else I know."

"You weren't exactly a Rambo either," Jimmy bristled.

"Somebody has to keep a watch, right?" Joe Rea asked mildly.

"Right," Keith agreed.

Jimmy looked from one to the other. "All right, what the heck, we will go."

The word "we" hadn't escaped Ronnie's attention. He cleared his throat and said, "I guess I deserved that."

The volunteers stepped into the light and onto a yard of white sand. Both tiptoed as if to sneak up on the house unnoticed.

* * *

The woods were alive with orbs.

"Are you sure they won't hurt us?" Keith asked with a nervous twitch.

"Sure, I'm sure. It's only energy."

"So is electricity!"

"Look, people have seen and studied orbs for years. No one has ever been hurt by one."

"That you know of."

* * *

Ronnie and Jimmy stood at the porch trying to up the nerve to climb steps.

Jimmy whispered, "You first."

The first step was half buried in dirt, the second one broken. Ronnie stretched his long leg to the third step and planted his right foot. "Push," Ronnie instructed his friends. Jimmy placed both hands on Ronnie's buttocks and shoved.

The swayed oak board squeaked under his weight. Stepping up to the creaky porch, Ronnie reached down to help his portly friend.

Next, Ronnie tiptoed over to the window and peeked in. Jimmy followed. Neither could see beyond the gritty pane.

"I can't see a thing," he whispered. "Too dark."

Jimmy saluted, forming a visor over his eyes. "I don't see anything either," he said, straightening up. "So, let's get outta this creepy place."

"May as well try the door while we're here," Ronnie said. He continued to whisper as if the house would hear him. He reached for the knob—and stopped. "What if someone lives here? That would explain the neat yard."

"And the weird music."

"But nobody does," Ronnie said. He sighed. "We're just trying to talk ourselves out of going in."

Grabbing the doorknob, Ronnie twisted.

Nothing. Ronnie released the breath he had been holding. "It's locked."

Relief washed over Jimmy's face. "Well, we tried, now let's go."

"Not yet. Come on, let's follow the porch around and see where it leads."

The porch wrapped around one side of the house, forming a breezeway. Two doors stood side by side that opened to the interior of the house. At the end of the breezeway a long, narrow, covered walkway extended to another building.

"I wonder what that leads to." Jimmy pointed toward the walkway.

"That's the summer kitchen," Ronnie explained. "That's another thing they did in the old days. The kitchen was separated from the main house to keep the heat out, but its main purpose was to save the house in case the kitchen caught fire. Crazy, huh?"

"No, that makes sense. We're crazy."

They stopped at the first door. "This is probably a bedroom." Ronnie gripped the rusty knob and held it. Jimmy closed his eyes. Ronnie turned the knob. Ca-lick. Ronnie jumped. Jimmy ran. He hit a post with a thwack and the porch shook. He held his nose while walking in circles. Blood dribbled off his chin, onto his shirt.

"Dude, you're seriously bleeding." Ronnie's whispered voice held an edge.

"No foolin'!"

"Here." Ronnie dug a crumpled handkerchief out of his back pocket. "Only slightly used. Hold your head back and pinch your nose."

After a few minutes the bleeding stopped. "Here, you can have your snot rag back." Jimmy shoved the blood-soaked hankie toward Ronnie.

Ronnie flung his hands up. "Oooh, dude, keep it!"

That's when they noticed the partially opened door. A shaft of light filtered to a narrow point on the bedroom floor. Darkness surrounded it.

Ronnie gave the door a slight push. It creaked open. Dim light from the globe covered the floor but stopped short of the far wall.

Ronnie said softly, "Come on, follow me."

Jimmy latched onto Ronnie's shirt and followed him in. A

drop of blood still oozed from Jimmy's nose.

The room was empty except for years of undisturbed dust. A door at the far end of the bedroom stood open.

Jimmy yanked on Ronnie's shirt. "Ain't this far enough?"

"What the heck, we're already in, may as well look around."

They stepped through the open door into the next room.

"Who-wee, stinks in here!" Jimmy said. He started to pinch his nostrils but thought better of it. The room smelled musty, like old dirt, the air stifling. No windows were in the inner room and light hadn't carried over from the bedroom's open door. The darkness was heavy.

Ronnie stiffened. "Something's wrong, feel it?"

Jimmy started to shake violently. "Th-th-there's s-s-something in here wi-wi-with us!"

Circles of light appeared throughout the room. "Orbs! Look, Jimmy, orbs! They're all around us!"

"We're gonna die, we're gonna die," Jimmy whimpered, turning to run.

An orb floated over the door. More appeared. Walls and ceiling were visible through the globes of light.

Jimmy whimpered again, "We're gonna die."

Ronnie uttered mewling sounds.

Orbs moved closer, changing shape, advancing.

"We're gonna die!" Jimmy repeated.

The orbs changed shapes. A large one in the corner, resembling a splatter on the wall, fashioned into the shape of a man.

"L-let's g-get outta here!" Ronnie shook the words out of his mouth. "Door, g-g-gotta f-f-find the d-door!"

Jimmy yanked Ronnie's shirt. Plink! A button hit the floor. A melon-sized orb floated overhead. The intruders dropped back, throwing their arms up. A human face materialized inside the orb. Lips formed the words, "Get out! Get out!"

The boys crouched.

Ronnie spotted the door. "Look!"

He rushed toward it. Jimmy clung to his shirt, and another button popped off.

A hand appeared, reached out, grabbed the doorknob and twisted it. The door flung open. The boys were sucked through the opening. They stumbled across the floor to the center of the room.

"L-look," Jimmy stammered, pointing to a phonograph sitting on an antique table. No other furniture occupied the room.

It began to play. A man in a rapper-style suit and brown fedora stood hunched over, hands crossed from one knee to the other. His whole body moved with the music.

A woman wearing oxblood red lipstick and a red flapper dress twirled a long strand of beads hanging from her neck. Her close-cropped hair was partially covered with a fitted, bell-shaped hat. Chandelier earrings dangled, sparkling. Her quick steps were in sync with the tinny music.

The music stopped. Static from the RCA went on for another few seconds.

Silence.

The man straightened up. The woman stood still and the flapper dress shimmied a few seconds longer.

"Listen, dudes, we're sorry," Ronnie squeaked. "We didn't mean anything, honest."

Plink! The last button popped off.

"Ye-yeah, th-that's right," Jimmy said. "W-we d-d-didn't mean anything."

The man and woman slowly turned their heads toward the two boys.

"Oh!" Ronnie mewled.

Their eyes were dead, void of light.

Jimmy crossed himself.

The dim, glowing light surrounding the house brightened as if someone had turned up the power.

The sightless couple stepped toward the boys.

Shadows danced on the walls as the glowing light grew brighter.

"Get out of there!" someone screamed, and pounded on the window.

Startled, Ronnie slammed against the wall. Jimmy went to his knees.

More pounding, more shouts. "Look, look!" Keith and Joe Rea hunkered at the window, arms animated, voices frantic. They watched orbs fill the room.

In the far corner a red, eye-shaped thing hovered near the planked ceiling. It drifted down toward Ronnie and Jimmy.

Grim faces materialized in all the orbs. They mouthed, "Get out! Get out!"

Keith ran around to the front door, grabbed the knob and rattled it.

Locked!

The macabre dancers moved closer, arms extended.

The shouting jolted Ronnie from his lethargic state. He grabbed Jimmy by the arms and tugged. "Get up," he pleaded.

The red orb pulsated, thumpa-thumpa-thumpa. The light grew bright, dim, bright, dim, with each thump.

It moved closer.

The flapper dress shimmied as the woman moved without touching the floor. The man tipped his hat.

Jimmy was on his feet. Ronnie held him steady.

Malevolent grins crossed the faces of the dancers.

"Run!" Ronnie pulled at Jimmy but he wouldn't budge.

Too late!

The two images reached out with open hands passing right through the boys. A cold chill saturated their bodies. Joe Rea banged on the window, rattling the dingy panes. The red orb floated across the room. Thumpa-thumpa-thumpa. Ronnie slapped Jimmy on the cheek, jarring him back to reality. The great orb moved toward the door, still at ceiling level. Thumpa-thumpa-thumpa. The boys dashed for the door. Both grabbed for the knob.

Jimmy wailed, “It’s locked!”

“Look, a key!” An old-fashioned keyhole held a long, slender skeleton key.

Ronnie grasped the flattened end between thumb and finger … turned it. Ca-lick!

Jimmy gripped the knob, turned and yanked. The door flung open. Keith fell forward and Jimmy caught him. Thumpa-thumpa-thumpa! The red orb dropped from the ceiling. Jimmy shoved Keith out the door, nearly pushing him down. Ronnie followed.

All four boys jumped from the porch at the same time. Jimmy hit the ground running, beating the other three to the road. The orb filled the doorway with its crimson spirit pulsing like a heartbeat. Thumpa-thumpa-thumpa!

Jimmy, running on adrenaline, didn’t slow down. His sizable frame heaved for breath as he led the way to the abandoned four-wheelers.

The glowing light dimmed when they reached the Recons. The forest orbs blinked out like fireflies.

With a leap, the four escapees straddled the seats.

They pressed the starters: re, re, ree … the engines burst to life.

“Yes!” they said, fists pumping.

The Hondas kicked sand in the air as they rounded the curve.

The boys lined up behind each other, their Recons hugging the narrow road. Keith, Joe Rea, Jimmy and Ronnie played tag as the four-wheelers nudged each other.

On the porch stood the man and woman, blank eyes staring, bodies stiff. Static blended with speakeasy music as the ATVs roared past the house and disappeared into the night.

DEMON EYES

Keith, Joe Rea, Ronnie and Jimmy pitched their tents on the banks of Mild Branch, a fast-running stream near their Five Points neighborhood.

"If the tent collapses around us in the middle of the night, it's Miller's fault," Joe Rea said, wiping his brow with his shirtsleeve. "Lame-o forgot to bring a hammer."

Ronnie shot back, "Stop whimpering, you have a rock, don'tcha?"

"Only one, but you have a head full." Joe Rea continued to drive tent stakes into the root-infested ground.

Keith looked around. "Where did Biggie get off to?"

"Right here." Jimmy stepped out of the pine thicket. "Went to find some firewood." He lowered his arms, and sticks and small branches clattered to the ground in a heap. Pieces of bark and sand clung to his sweaty pullover.

Joe Rea placed a tent stake inside the loop and stretched it back. The palm-sized rock clunked the stake point into the ground.

"Hey, Biggie," Ronnie said, peering from inside the tent, "what are the palmetto spears for?"

"Marshmallows. Stopped at the S&S for a couple of bags. Thought we could roast them later tonight."

Joe Rea dropped his rock and his mouth began to quiver. "Ma-ma-marshmallows? Did you say marsh-mallows?" He grabbed his stomach, he-hawing like a jackass. When he finally stifled the laughing he said, "Hey, guys, Biggie Redmon brought marshmallows. We're gonna sit by the fire and sing 'Kum Ba Yah'."

Ronnie, kneeling inside the tent while straightening the tent pole, snickered and said, “Hey, Biggie, we gonna hold hands while we sway back and forth?”

Snickers turned to hoots.

“Fine, go ahead, laugh, you ingrates, I’ll eat ’em all myself. And stop calling me Biggie!”

Keith said, “Hey, Biggie, um, I mean Jimmy.” He stopped digging the fire pit and leaned on his shovel. “You didn’t hear me laugh, didja? So you can share with me, right? I looove ma-ma-marrsh…” The corner of his mouth quivered. He glanced at the others, fell to his knees and cackled hysterically.

Joe Rea doubled over and howled. Ronnie rolled out of the tent, hands clasped around his belly, hooting and hawing. Keith wallowed teary-eyed in the fire pit.

Jimmy kicked the pile of kindling. “Go ahead and have your hoo-rahs. Hope Demon Eyes getcha!”

Keith stopped laughing. “Did you say Demon Eyes?”

“Yeah, you know,” Jimmy retorted, “the green-eyed monster from the swamp, remember? Babysitters and older kids threatened to throw us to Demon Eyes if we didn’t behave.”

“Worked for me,” Joe Rea said.

“Me too.” Ronnie bounced to his feet and brushed sticky pine needles from his clothes. “I haven’t thought about ol’ Demon Eyes for a long time. What made you think about it, Biggie?”

“That’s what my brother, Nick, used to say, ‘Hope Demon Eyes getcha,’ when I’d piss him off about something.”

“You know,” Ronnie said, “some of the old folk around here claim they’ve seen it. I even heard old man Lawrence say so with my own ears—claimed he’d been chased by it.”

It all came back to the boys in a flood of childhood memories: the stories of the legendary little monster that lived in Andrew’s Swamp. They recalled tales of its thundering hooves as it galloped over open fields, its bright green eyes that glowed in the dark—the madder it became, the brighter its eyes glowed. People said it was a creature possessed by demons from hell.

Keith scooped a shovelful of dirt from the fire pit and then leaned on the handle. "My Granddaddy Bennett, if you can believe this, says he saw it a couple of months back while walking on the edge of the swamp. He got an attitude when I acted like I didn't believe him."

"Well, maybe he did see it," Jimmy said. "He is your granddaddy, for crying out loud. Why wouldn't you believe him?"

"Maybe you're right … heeeey!" Keith kicked the shovel point into the dirt and smiled.

"Uh-oh, I don't like that look." Jimmy shook his head from shoulder to shoulder. "The answer is no. N-O!"

Joe Rea slapped his hands together, saying, "I'm in."

"Yeah." Ronnie smacked Jimmy on the shoulder and said, "Us too."

"Whaddya mean *us*?" Jimmy shoved Ronnie away. "Don't you understand a simple word like NO?"

"Aw, come on," Ronnie said, "it'll be fun."

"Have you forgotten about the railroad tracks where we barely escaped being chopped to pieces by a phantom train, or the old house with the highly pissed orbs—huh, have you? Well, I haven't!" Jimmy crossed his arms. "Now you wanna let a green-eyed monster eat us for supper. No thanks!"

The boys knew he would come around eventually, he always did. Jimmy knew he would too. However, he felt obligated to voice his strong opposition to any and everything that might bite, gouge, maim, scare or threaten in any way. His friends expected it.

The hot, sweaty teens finished setting up camp. They were drenched down with sweat and decided the weather much too hot for a campfire, so they popped the top on cans of Beanie Weenies, ripped open bags of Doritos and slurped Cokes retrieved from the ice-packed Playmate. They ate like kings.

"Wow!" said Joe Rea. "How sweet is this?"

Sienna shades of light produced long shadows that danced as a bright red sun set beyond the canopy of yellow pine. A mixture of sweet earth, pine straw and wildflowers formed an aromatic tonic saturating the warm air. The gurgling sound of sparkling mirror waters flowed against low creek banks and over a fallen tree that no longer offered shade. So far it had been a perfect day.

"Wow!" Joe Rea said again. "How sweet is this?"

Coke and Sprite clanked against each other as they landed in the trash along with clattery Doritos bags and shredded candy wrappers.

Jimmy, ready to burn some marshmallows, kneeled at the fire pit and lit a match. Keith blew it out.

"Hey, why didja do that for?" Jimmy said, giving Keith a gentle shove.

"Hey, watch the tender bod, bro," Keith said after catching his balance. "Didn't we agree to hold off on the fire until it cooled down—and after we returned from hunting ol' Demon Eyes?"

"Geez." Jimmy's shoulders slumped. "I'd hoped you had forgotten your crazy idea of … aahh, what the heck, let's go."

Keith gave him a quick jab in the shoulder and said, "Awesome, dude!"

Joe Rea smiled and stuck both thumbs up.

"Yes!" Ronnie pumped a fist in the air. "The Spook Club rides again!"

Recons with the Honda wing trademark emblazoned on the gas tanks sat ready to travel. The boys donned their helmets and straddled the black seats. With a touch of the starter and some wee-wee-weee-va-rooommmm, the four-stroke engines jumped to life.

No road led to or from the campsite. The four-wheelers weaved around trees and clumps of palmetto and plowed through brush. The convoy resembled a snake with bobbing headlights.

"Aaaah!" Ronnie hollered.

His four-wheeler slammed into a tree and stopped. Jumping off the stalled Recon, Ronnie ran in circles, yelling hysterically and slapping the air.

"Spider, spider!" He beat his ears to a blood red and attacked his hair with relentless brutality. "Get it off, get it off!"

"Dude," Joe Rea shouted, "you gone crazy or something?"

"Rabies, he's got rabies," Jimmy yelled. "A rabid spider done bit 'im."

Keith rolled his eyes. "You don't get rabies from spiders, stupid."

Ronnie jumped in front of a headlight, still dancing a jig. "You see a spider anywhere? Do you? Get it off me!" He continued to slap himself silly.

"There ain't no spider on you, dude, just some web, that's all." Keith held his stomach and laughed. "You're not scared of an itty-bitty spider, are you?"

"Durn straight I am! I'm terrified of the little blood-sucking monsters." Calming down, Ronnie pulled sticky web from his hair.

Everybody had a good laugh while Ronnie inspected his Recon. "Darn! Double darn! My fender's all dented and scratched up."

"You didn't hurt the poor spider, didja?" Joe Rea teased. "If you did, I'm gonna turn you in for spider abuse."

"Shove it!" Ronnie let his left hand slide down his right arm as he shoved upward.

Jimmy grinned. "I still say he has rabies."

"You're both hilarious, ha-ha." Ronnie pulled the last remnants of web from his hair. "Come on, clowns, let's go."

The four riders negotiated the forest landscape without disturbing any more spiders or having another ear-slapping, hair-pulling episode.

The Recons scrambled from the woods, on to Gum Swamp Road. Knobby tires sang over rough pavement. Gum

Swamp Road soon merged at the Point. Gum Swamp, Double Run Road, Highway 41 and old Highway 441 met together, forming the southern boundary of Five Points. The demon hunters crossed to old 441, then headed north. The five-mile stretch of rough cement was an obsolete and seldom-used road connecting at the north end of Five Points to the new and improved Highway 441.

The adventurous teens were alone on the five-mile stretch of broken pavement, headlights carving a luminous tunnel through the night. Shadows danced at the edges of the road, waiting impatiently for the red-winged vehicles to pass.

The boys and their machines approached the turnoff leading them to the swamp road. Keith led the pack. He touched the brake pedal, flashing a red warning to the three riders behind him. One by one they left the pavement and bounced onto the narrow, rutty trail.

Keith, Jimmy, Joe Rea, and Ronnie shifted the Recons into low gear, allowing the machines to growl over the uneven terrain.

Keith called back, "Not long now, we're getting close."

"Too close, if you ask me," Jimmy mumbled to himself.

After about a hundred more yards of slow growling over uneven land and deep mud holes, Keith squeezed the clutch and shifted into neutral.

"This is it," Keith said, "Andrew's Swamp, home of Demon Eyes."

In a monotone, Jimmy said, "Whoop-ee."

The teens positioned their Hondas so their headlamps could shine down the narrow, washed-out road.

Gazing into the swamp, Ronnie sounded doubtful: "You call that a road?"

"Perfect place to get eaten by wild beasts or swallared by giant snakes," Jimmy said as he wrenched off his helmet and gazed down the muddy trail. "You don't expect me to go down there, do you?"

Ronnie clicked the headlamp to BRIGHT. "Geez, the road—if that's what you call it—looks totally ratty."

"A rat wouldn't survive in that cesspool, for crissakes," Jimmy whined. "'Sides, I don't know why we can't wait until morning so we can see where we're going."

"What fun is that?" Keith asked. "I mean, come on, Biggie, don't be such a wimp."

"Yeah … don't be such a wimp," Joe Rea repeated. "You comin' or not?"

"You know I am."

"Okay then, quit gripin' and let's go." Joe Rea gave a flip of his hand, motioning toward the washed-out road. "Why don't you lead us through, Biggie?"

"I said I'd go, I didn't say I'd be the sacrificial lamb." Jimmy pointed to Keith. "'Sides, this was his brilliant idea, let him lead."

Everybody stared at Keith, who shrugged his shoulders and said, "No problema, let's go."

Keith popped the transmission into first gear, causing the Honda to lurch. He eased out the clutch and the ATV growled into the entrance of Andrew's Swamp. Jimmy, Joe Rea and Ronnie followed.

* * *

Crickets as dense as the population of China chirped in perfect harmony, accompanied by bass-crooning bullfrogs and tiny soprano singing tree frogs. Cypress trees with gray stringy bark and twisted moss imitated old men with beards. An owl hooted.

Something leapt from the undergrowth. Keith slammed on brakes.

Jimmy swerved and nose-dived his Recon to a halt. Joe Rea and Ronnie slid precariously in opposite directions.

A black panther stood blocking the road. Its ears lowered and flattened against its head. A throaty growl rolled out of the cat's mouth. It crouched, snarled, then leapt.

"Aaaaahhhh!" Arm shields flew up.

The big cat bounded in front of Keith's ATV. Its sleek body stretched, flexing its powerful muscles. Wild, steely eyes glowered in the headlight. It hunkered down and snarled.

Keith shouted, "Oh, crap!"

White fangs reflected in the artificial light.

Jimmy yelled, "We're gonna die! We're gonna die!"

The cat's mighty head turned sideways. It lifted a paw.

"Back up!" Ronnie yelled.

Frantically the riders clicked into reverse and twisted the throttle—too fast. The riders met in a tangled Honda menagerie with no way to escape.

The cat squalled like a terrified woman.

"Aaaaahhhh! Aaaaahhhh!" the boys shrieked.

The cat sprang.

* * *

Deep in the swamp, Demon Eyes stirred. The terrifying scream of the big cougar and the frightened cries of the teenagers put it on high alert. Wild, nervous eyes scanned the swampland. Then something inside the beast awakened. Fury swirled through its senses. Anger grew from an inner source, fueling its eyes to a bright demon green.

With a snap of its head, the body followed and Demon Eyes scurried through dense brush, its glowing eyes illuminating the way.

* * *

"Come on, Biggie, snap out of it." Ronnie tried prying Jimmy's hands from the handlebar but he refused to relinquish his grip. He sat scrunched over the seat with his face pushed against the gas tank.

"I can't believe that panther jumped right over us," Keith said, trying to get his shaking body under control.

"And that scream!" Joe Rea recalled. "It was awesome!"

"Sounded like a woman screaming," Ronnie said.

"Yeah, kinda like the way we sounded," Keith said with a weak laugh. "I expect we scared the pee out of that poor little kitty."

Ronnie nudged Jimmy. "Geez, would you get up already?"

Little by little Jimmy eased his grip.

"Am I dead?" With caution Jimmy opened one eye and peeked around. Convinced he was still among the living he sat up and then patted his face and chest. "I can't believe I'm in one piece."

"Don't worry," Ronnie assured him, "you're still alive and wimpy."

"I plan to stay alive and wimpy, too. I'm getting my wimpy ass outta here as quick as I can get this thing turned around."

"For cryin' out loud, Biggie," Ronnie wailed, "it was only a cat."

"A cat? Only a cat, you say? It was a friggin' lion, for crissakes!"

"Go then." Ronnie bowed and gestured toward the swamp's entrance. "But that lion ran back thataway. It's probably in a tree somewhere just waiting to tear your head off."

"Crap!" Jimmy's ashen face turned even paler. "Why I continually let you sick wackos talk me into these crazy and always near fatal exploits of yours, I'll never understand!" Defeated, he pushed the START, reigniting the stalled engine. "Well, what are we waitin' for, let's get this over with."

* * *

Demon Eyes slipped into the murky, foul-smelling water and with squatty legs swam from one island to the other. Its eyes burned a bright emerald. Something had invaded its territory. Guttural sounds stemmed from its short throat. Harsh grunts became increasingly louder and stronger as it ripped through water hyacinth and snake-infested waters.

* * *

Sixteen wheels rolled through sticky black muck, caking tires and fender wells. The road had gotten worse.

Keith held up his hand and pressed the brake. The taillight flashed STOP. "Looks radical up ahead," he said. "Should we chance it?"

Jimmy spoke first. "Let's see, hmmm, man-eating cat behind us, instant death. Up ahead a little mud on our shoes … no brainer, bro. I'll take my chances with the mud. 'Sides," he patted the gas tank, "these babies are made for this kind of travel."

"He's right for a change," Joe Rea said. "We've come this far, so why go back now? I think we're almost through anyway."

"I think he's right," Ronnie agreed. "We're probably only a couple of hundred yards shy of the other side."

With throttles eased open, the ATVs crept forward, past moss-laden cypress trees. Bullfrogs startled by the approaching Recons leapt into the putrid water, pushing off with a swoosh.

"There's a big one up ahead," Keith shouted back. "I don't know how deep it is and there's no way around it."

A yawning mud hole completely covered the eight-foot passageway.

Keith eased his four-wheeler into thick sluice. The knobby tires gradually sank to its hubs but kept going. About midway through, water inched up to meet the footboards. Keith lifted his feet trying to protect his Nikes from the muddy water.

Without warning the rear tires lost traction in the slick mud and slid sideways into a drop-off. The left footboard submerged. Keith lost his balance. Instantly his white Nike plunged into the filthy water and hit the footboard. His foot braced against it, stopping his fall. He gunned the throttle. The tires spun, throwing mud and water into the air.

Catching solid ground again, the four-wheeler lurched up the opposite bank onto dry ground.

Keith stopped and looked back. The others sat waiting.

"Well, what are you waitin' for?" Keith asked.

"They were just waiting to see if you would drown," Jimmy said, nudging his thumb over his shoulder toward Joe Rea and Ronnie. Looking back he said, "So, you comin' or not?" He turned the throttle and the Recon slipped into the water. The other two followed.

* * *

Demon Eyes burrowed its way through walls of briers and clumps of saw palmetto. Its chest heaved with fury, causing its eyes to grow hotter and brighter as it moved closer to the invaders.

* * *

All four boys' feet were soaked, causing their socks to squeak in their shoes that responded to each bump and dip. Their ATVs, covered with thick gumbo, plowed along negotiating every perilous mud hole and runnel on the washed-out road.

Keith's eyes grew large. "Snake!" he screamed, and braced for the impact.

Too late. The cottonmouth struck. Its fangs hammered a thud into the left fender. It recoiled quickly, tongue darting in and out. The front tires hit the moccasin and the huge snake rolled underneath the carriage. The rear wheels grabbed it, flinging it backward into Jimmy's ATV.

"Eee-yaaaa!" Jimmy gunned the throttle.

The serpent's mouth gaped open. The Honda's headlight glared into the cotton-white mouth. Thumpty-thumpty! The huge snake pummeled the undercarriage. Suddenly the wheels slung it to the side of the road.

Joe Rea sighted the moccasin in his headlight, the head flattened and poised to strike.

"Oh, crap!" He threw his legs up.

It struck … missed.

Ronnie slammed on brakes and slid to a stop. He jerked his leg up. The snake turned and struck, hitting the footboard. The cottonmouth recoiled. Its eyes glared cold and deadly. Its tongue flickered. Its head flattened out. Ronnie lost his balance, landing in the sticky mud with a splat.

The Recon lunged forward and died.

The snake recoiled for another strike. A dark mass came to life and its jaws separated and clamped down on the unsuspecting cottonmouth.

Together, Keith, Jimmy and Joe Rea shouted, "Gator! Gator!"

The old bull gator backed into the water, disappearing into its hole.

Ronnie, covered with mud, leapt to his feet and bounded onto the seat. He squeezed the clutch and hit the starter at the same time. The engine sprang to life. He twisted the throttle and popped the clutch. The Recon's front wheels momentarily left the ground as the rear tires propelled it forward.

* * *

Growls, low and lingering, slid from the throat of the demon-eyed fiend. Its legs, short and stout, pumped frantically. Green eyes flashed. Its head turned from side to side searching, a slobbery tongue wagging as the beast thundered faster and faster toward its target.

* * *

Clearly shaken, the boys trudged along. Their close encounter with the panther, the snake and the bull gator had taken their toll on the weary trekkers.

"We're almost through," Keith yelled back. "I think we're

at the edge of the swamp."

Jimmy formed praying hands. "Thank you, Jesus!"

A large clearing stood stark and empty at the edge of the swamp. The four teens pulled off the road into the spacious field. Their headlights revealed an abundance of pink-tipped rabbit weed with green stems. The north and west sides of the meadow formed an L-shape where a forest of yellow pine grew amidst clumps of palmetto. On the south side of the clearing the swamp formed a ragged boundary of moss-covered conifers and bald cypress knees standing in black, murky water.

"Tell me again why we risked our lives to trudge through this hellhole?" Jimmy asked. "And geez, look at my once beautiful four-wheeler. It'll take hours of intense labor to get this sticky muck off."

"Adventure," Keith said. "Admit it, you had fun."

"Totally awesome," Joe Rea said, swinging his arms down like two hammers. "We met danger and spit in its eye."

"Yeah, well, I got mud in my eye," Ronnie said. "Not to mention my hair, arms—"

"And you stink, too." Keith held his nose. "Whew!"

"Yeah, well, I resign from the Spook Club." Jimmy's voice held a determined edge. "This is the last time you clowns are gonna talk me into anything. Really, this is it!"

Joe Rea looked at Keith and Ronnie. "All in favor of Biggie being president, say yes."

"Yes!" they yelled together.

"It's unanimous." Joe Rea grabbed Jimmy's hand and shook it. "Congratulations, Mr. President."

"Screw you!" Jimmy pulled his hand free to wild applause.

The field, outlined by dark forest and swamp, seemed bright in comparison. The clear night sky raining starlight from the mysterious Milky Way added a measure of comfort to the mud-soaked boys standing by their silent machines.

The stillness broke.

Birds whirled from their roosts in a massive rush.

The boys jumped and gazed skyward.

The swamp came alive. Bushes swayed and the ground shook.

The boys struggled to discern the noise.

Throaty grunts and heavy breathing accompanied the pounding of something running.

Keith, Joe Rea, Jimmy and Ronnie froze in steeped fear.

The swamp blazed with a green glow. Demon Eyes came with a fury.

The boys stood like statues, eyes wide and hearts fluttering.

It burst into the open and splashed through shallow water at the swamp's edge.

Jimmy made mewing sounds.

Green eyes blazed and bobbled up and down as short powerful legs thrust Demon Eyes toward the static invaders.

Like a sudden slap in the face the boys came to life.

Demon Eyes closed in.

"Jump!" Keith shouted and bounded feet first onto the Recon's seat. Ronnie and Joe Rea did the same.

Jimmy leapt, missed and fell flat on the ground.

Demon Eyes shot straight for the prone intruder.

Keith, Joe Rea and Ronnie pleaded, "Get up! Get up!"

Jimmy grabbed the footboard and pulled to his knees.

The throaty grunts grew louder.

"Come on! Come on!" They screamed louder, "Hurry! Hurry!"

Jimmy could feel its hot breath. Reaching, he grabbed the handlebar and pulled. He was on his feet.

Demon Eyes rammed into Jimmy's legs and he fell forward, slamming into the gas tank.

"Aaaaaah! Over here!" The boys jumped from their seats, arms waving frantically, taunting, "Over here! Over here!"

Demon Eyes churned around and dashed toward the

animated intruders. Jimmy managed to pull himself up, rolling onto the seat.

Keith and Ronnie scrambled to the seats of the four-wheelers. Standing, they continued to wave and yell.

With a wham, Joe Rea was down.

Demon Eyes stopped, backed up and with blazing eyes examined his prey. It rolled its head from side to side, snarling, studying. Its mouth opened, exposing needle-thin teeth. Its hair bristled on its back like a wild boar's. It took a step.

Joe Rea crabbed backward.

Keith and Ronnie were now on the ground, shouting, waving and trying to draw attention from their downed friend.

Demon Eyes didn't notice.

Joe Rea pushed against the ATV.

Jimmy kneeled on the Recon's seat, head down and butt sticking in the air.

Joe Rea tried desperately to get up. He touched his cheek to the hot engine. "Oh!" He recoiled, grabbing his face.

Demon Eyes lunged, wrapped its mouth around Joe Rea's Air Jordan and scampered backward. Joe Rea followed, sliding along on his back.

Immediately Keith and Ronnie grabbed Joe Rea by his wrists and pulled in the opposite direction.

The powerful creature wasn't fazed. It grunted, increasing its speed. Keith and Ronnie tried to hold on. They stumbled, fell and were dragged along. Still, they managed to hold on.

"Oh! Ouch!" The sharp teeth dug into his foot. He pleaded, "Don't let go, please!"

Demon Eyes increased its speed. The hair on its back stood straight up. It grunted with each breath. The boys hung on. Joe Rea's arms were stretched to the limit.

Ronnie and Keith lost their grip.

Demon Eyes dragged its prey to the edge of the swamp.

Wham! Jimmy kicked Demon Eyes in the head. It

released its grip on Joe Rea's foot. Wham! Jimmy kicked it again, this time in the ribs.

Demon Eyes left the ground, landing on its side. Quickly it rolled to its feet. Its eyes blazed. Throaty growls belched from its gullet. Its mouth twisted in a snarl. Joe Rea's blood dripped from pointy teeth.

Ronnie and Jimmy scurried to their feet and yanked on Joe Rea's still-outstretched arms. Shoving with his heels, Joe Rea ripped clumps from the muddy earth.

Demon Eyes lunged at Jimmy.

A blood-curdling scream pierced the night. The black panther leapt from a low branch onto the back of Demon Eyes.

Joe Rea shot to his feet, tried to run … couldn't. Keith and Ronnie grabbed him by his arms and pulled him toward the Recons. Jimmy lumbered behind them.

The cat roared. Demon Eyes screeched with madness. They rolled, bit and slapped their paws at each other. Then the little monster zigzagged into the swamp.

The cat turned and looked at the boys, let out a low growl and then bounded into the slough.

* * *

The wet and muddy adventurers pulled over at an S&S to take advantage of the bright lights. Joe Rea sat on the side of the Recon's seat and gingerly pulled his Air Jordan off his damaged foot.

"Oh crap, look at that!" Joe Rea dangled his bloody sock by two fingers and then dropped it beside his shredded shoe.

"Geez," Jimmy said, "looks like a bloody pin cushion. Hope you don't start foaming at the mouth or something."

"Hey Keith," Ronnie said, "I think you should apologize to your grandfather."

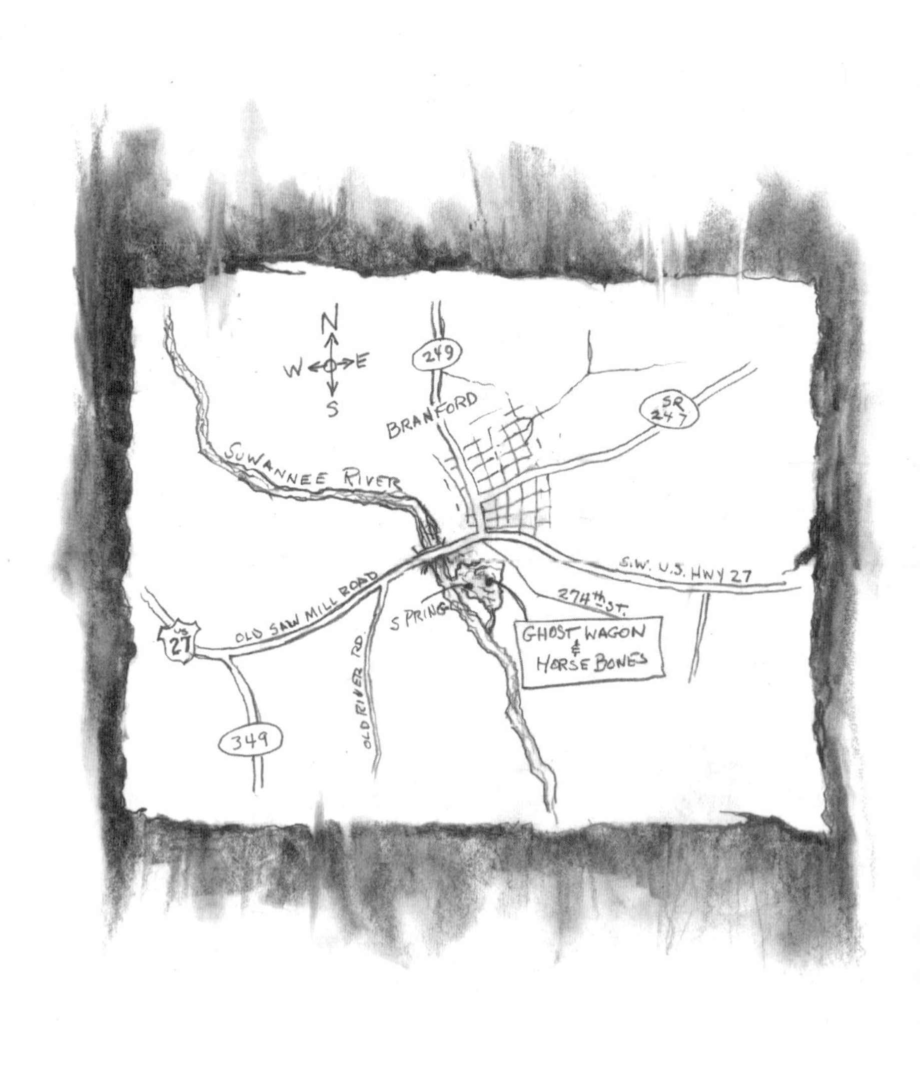
N
W
E
S
249
BRANFORD
SR 247
SUWANNEE RIVER
S.W. U.S. HWY 27
274th ST.
OLD SAW MILL ROAD
US 27
OLD RIVER RD.
SPRING
GHOST WAGON & HORSE BONES
349

GHOST WAGON AND HORSE BONES

In 1840, pioneers settled on the banks of the pristine Suwannee River in North Florida, in an area that would later become the town of Branford. The Suwannee, *Swani* in Cherokee, means Echo River. Wide and deep, the river flows lazily on its journey to the Gulf of Mexico. On the east side of the river where the settlement began, there boiled a clear, cold spring flowing directly into the tea-colored waters of the fabled river.

Late one stormy afternoon, something awful happened.

* * *

1840

George Walker's camp, located about two hundred feet from the spring, consisted of a one-room cabin and a corral. George, having gathered wood for fuel, stopped the wagon in front of his cabin, jumped down and began to unload. In his haste he forgot to set the brake.

It had been a calm day. Wood smoke from campfires wisped dreamlike through heavy air. Then a rapid change occurred. Smoke swirled and churned, ashes and embers flew in every direction.

A thunderstorm brewed. Wind flapped through trees and thunder tumbled across a darkened sky. Gonda's ears pricked and the great draft horse stamped a foot and whinnied.

"Easy boy, calm down," George said soothingly to the Belgian. George unloaded and stacked the wood, trying to beat the storm.

Ominous clouds, dark with rain, grew into boiling mountains.

Angry thunder grumbled like old men. With ears twitching and eyes anxious, Gonda looked back at George. The Belgian quick-stepped, jerking the wagon.

"Whoa, now—easy, fella," George said calmly to the horse. "Steady, boy, almost through."

The draft horse descended from a proud breed that once carried armored knights into battle during medieval times. His name meant Noble Warrior, and he looked the part, standing seventeen hands high. His regal head resembled an ornament atop a powerfully built body bred to work in the fields and pull heavy loads.

Chestnut in color, Gonda wore a blond mane and tail, and blond socks dressed his muscular legs. A striking blaze ran from head to nose. He could smell the rain. His mane, charged by the electrified atmosphere, danced about.

A bolt of lightning ripped through the clouds, splitting a pine tree in two. Gonda bolted. The wagon gave chase, bouncing over uneven terrain. The remaining firewood plummeted to the ground, leaving a jagged trail.

The spring lay in Gonda's path. Too late! Turning a hard right, the spooked animal tried to stop. The wagon slid, dropping the wheels over the edge and flipping it into freezing water. The big steed lost his footing. He kicked and jerked trying to regain a foothold. No use; the wagon's momentum yanked him backward into the spring. Water rushed over the banks, horse and wagon sank in slow motion, landing on the brink of the cave some thirty feet below.

George ran to the spring. Others followed. Together they watched helplessly as Gonda kicked and bucked in an attempt to break free of the wagon. George dove into the roiling water, along with several others, in an attempt to save the trapped animal.

They didn't succeed. Gonda gave up the battle for life and drifted to the sandy bottom. Resting on his side, he remained hitched to the wagon. Trace lines, like ghostly arms, stirred from the cave's flowing water.

That's the way George described it, and the story has survived for over a hundred and sixty years. The old-timers in Branford swear they've seen the wagon on the bottom of the spring on moonlit nights. The skeletal remains of the great draft horse, they say, are still yoked to its collar, neck vertebrae extending through it. The harness and trace rings, they claim, lie over the bones and the reins rest on the wagon seat, gently swaying with the flow of the spring.

* * *

2007

"Come on, let's go," Randy Hatch pleaded. His tall frame towered over Keith Dampier, Joe Rea Phillips, Jimmy Redmon and Ronnie Miller. "I'm seriously ready to dive into some cool H2O."

The boys were gathered at Joe Rea's house in Five Points, a working-class neighborhood north of Lake City, Florida.

"Hey, lookit, Biggie's wearing a bathing suit." Keith snickered at the sight. "Swimsuit, bro, a swimsuit? Be serious. Cutoffs is what you wear to swim in, not a sissy bathing suit, for chrissakes."

"Totally uncool," Ronnie agreed.

"Nerdy," Randy said.

"Geeky," Joe Rea said, completing the list of insults.

"Shove it where the sun don't shine," Jimmy countered with an upward motion of his finger. "Shove it way up!"

"We goin' to the river?" Ronnie asked.

"How about Branford Springs?" Randy suggested. "You can ride over with me. We can set up camp on my place and hit the springs tonight."

Everybody nodded in agreement.

"Can we go skinny-dippin'?" Joe Rea asked. "Otherwise somebody might see Biggie's bathing suit and think we're city slickers. Wouldn't want to be embarrassed."

"Hey guys," Jimmy said, pointing at Joe Rea's crotch, "you think my bathing suit's embarrassing, wait till you see him with his clothes off. Can't tell him from a girl."

Hoots, hollers and knee-slapping went on for a while. Jimmy grinned at the clever come-back.

"Up yours, Biggie," Joe Rea shot back.

"Hey, they don't call me Biggie for nothin'." Jimmy felt prouder by the minute.

With that exchange, everybody unlatched cell phones to call or text their parents for permission to go on the overnighter. Their parents knew and trusted each other and were used to the frequent sleepovers and camping trips during summer break.

All five piled into Randy's beat-up Trans Am. Jimmy took the front bucket while Keith, Ronnie and Joe Rea squeezed into the backseat.

Keith stuck his head around Randy's cracked leather bucket and said, "So bro, tell us about the spring."

"It's wet." Randy glanced around and smiled.

"Smart butt," Keith shot back. "You know what I mean."

"It's cold." Randy threw up a hand. "Okay, okay! It's right on the edge of the river. The boil has formed a nice-sized pool and the water from there flows straight to the river. … Answer your question?"

Before Keith could reply, Randy added, "Oh, one other thing, it's haunted."

"Haunted?" Ronnie leaned forward. "How can a spring be haunted?"

Randy related the sad story about the great Belgian horse. The boys huddled as close to the driver as possible, giving him their full attention.

"I've worked in my dad's Western Auto store since I was a kid," Randy said. "I've heard people, especially the old folks, say they've actually seen the wagon and the skeleton of the horse at the bottom of the spring."

Joe Rea drawled out, "Cool."

"Awesome," Keith said as a wry smile crossed his face.

"Sweet," Ronnie joined in, then looked at Jimmy and grinned.

"Oh crap, here we go again!" Jimmy slumped down in the seat and sighed.

Randy, puzzled, shot Jimmy a glance, then looked at the others. "What?"

"Wanna join the Spook Club?" Keith asked. "It's very exclusive, you know."

"Yeah," Jimmy piped up. "Only idiots are allowed to join."

* * *

The Trans Am clattered over the rutty dirt road leading to the Hatch property just east of Branford Springs. The sprawling farm consisted mostly of pasture land for grazing cattle. Several acres were planted in corn, peas and butterbeans. Ears of Silver Queen corn, with dark blonde tassels drooping from green shuck, were about ready to harvest.

Jimmy clambered out of the tightly packed Pontiac, unlatched the gate and swung it open. Randy pressed the gas. … The car sputtered and popped. Tapping the gas pedal gently, the engine caught, sending the barely living jalopy lurching through the gate.

An old barn sat alone in the middle of the field, its tin roof brown with rust. Boards cracked from hard years were covered with faded red paint. Two corroded signs nailed to the side of one wall read "Wayne Feeds" and "Mail Pouch Tobacco."

"Hayloft okay to sleep in?" Randy asked.

"Hayloft?" Keith brightened up. "Any females around we can invite? I would love to roll in the hay with a nubile young maiden."

"And go skinny-dippin' with them in the spring," Joe Rea joined in.

"You'd have to wear my bathing suit so we wouldn't be embarrassed." Jimmy looked at Joe Rea's crotch and grinned.

That constituted a knee-slapper. Randy went to his knees and Ronnie rolled around on his back. Keith fell against the barn door and slid to the ground, holding his stomach. The hoots went on for a while.

"Funny, ha-ha," Joe Rea said, and kicked a rusty bucket. "Go ahead and laugh. … I'll get you for that one, Biggie."

"I've worked up an appetite," Jimmy said after they were all laughed out. "What we havin' for supper?"

"I'll tell you what you can have for supper," Joe Rea said, shaking his fist. "A knuckle sandwich, that's what!"

"How about Beenie's weenies," Jimmy howled, ignoring the fist.

That brought on another round of hoots and knee-slapping.

You could almost see steam coming from Joe Rea's head.

"Fine!" he said.

Randy swung the barn door open. The teens were greeted by a green John Deere tractor with a set of harrows still connected to the three-point hitch. Stalls lined both sides of the barn. Just beyond, a ladder led to the hayloft.

"We'll get our things up to the loft, then we'll build us a campfire and roast some weenies."

A gaggle of laughs erupted. Immediately Randy realized what he had said. Looking at Joe Rea, he made a sudden and wise decision not to laugh.

* * *

"It's hot," Keith said while wiping his brow. "I don't know about you, but I'm ready for a swim in the haunted spring."

"Now?" Jimmy sounded incredulous. "It's dark, in case you haven't noticed."

"So? The water's still wet, ain't it?" Ronnie cracked.

"Besides," Joe Rea added, "the moon's out, we should

have plenty of light to swim by. … Hey, you don't believe that stuff about the wagon, do you?"

"Who, me? Believe in a ghost wagon?" Jimmy rolled his eyes. "No more than I believe in haunted houses with orbs or railroad spikes that appear mysteriously, ghost kids or demon-eyed beasts. Heck no, not me!" Jimmy's previous encounters with the supernatural had left him skeptical when it came to so-called legends. So far they had all turned out to be real.

All five crammed inside the almost dead Trans Am and headed toward the spring with windows down … the air conditioner already dead. Warm wind whipped through open windows, fluttering pullover shirts. Randy's blond locks thrashed about his face and half covered his eyes. Jimmy looked at him wryly, ready to grab the wheel if a crash seemed imminent. The moon sat just above the horizon, lighting up the countryside with its radiant beams.

"Here we are," Randy announced.

All five boys fell out of the cramped rattletrap.

In the distance the glow of the little town looked quaint and peaceful. The river glistened, its flow unimpeded under the great bridge on its journey to the Gulf of Mexico. Water burbled where it escaped from the deep cave, and then snaked swiftly from the pool to the river.

"Last one in is a fairy," Keith shouted. He scampered to the spring's edge, made a quick assessment and dove in head first. Joe Rea, Ronnie and Randy followed in quick succession. Jimmy, the fairy, ambled down to the spring's edge and stuck his foot into the clear cold water.

"Geez! I ain't getting in that freezing stuff," Jimmy announced. "A polar bear wouldn't survive in that."

"Neither do chickens, evidently," Randy said, treading water. He tried to cluck but trill sounds came out instead.

Jimmy held his ground while the other four remained in the ice-cold spring, mouths quivering, dimpled skin turning a light shade of blue. Keith, Joe Rea and Randy wanted to get out, to feel the warmth of the July night … bask in the humidity … to sweat again. But no one wanted to be the first to admit how cold they really were. At least, they all thought with admiration, that Jimmy had been honest. He stood there with nothing to prove, warm and dry.

The water shimmied into a dream-like state. Images began to appear on the sandy bottom.

Jimmy blinked, not believing what he was seeing. He leaned forward, scrunching his eyes for a better look. The image became clear. “What the—”

“Jump in and get it over with,” Randy called out, his lips a dark blue. “It ain’t that cold.”

Jimmy straightened up. His mouth hung open.

“You okay, dude?” Randy asked, noticing the confused look on Jimmy’s face.

“Look at th-that!” Jimmy pointed toward the turbulent water.

Randy gazed in the direction of Jimmy’s trembling finger. “Oh, crap!” Like a rabbit he headed for dry land, while yelling, “Get out! Now!”

Arms and legs went wild, clambering to get out.

Jimmy continued to point.

“It’s a friggin’ wagon!” Ronnie said, bending over to get a better look.

All five boys gawked at the wagon, its front wheels turned at an angle, the hitch dangling trace rings.

Something else lay on the spring’s bottom.

“Well, I’ll be,” Joe Rea whispered. “A horse, that’s what it is. It’s the skeleton of a friggin’ horse.”

Keith drawled, “I’ll be durned if it ain’t!”

The clear water waved in dream-like fashion revealing the skeleton of a horse. A bridle with black and cracked leather nuzzled around a bleached skull connected by vertebrae. The rib cage lay prominently beside great leg bones.

“They were telling the truth …”

All eyes focused on Randy.

He said, "The old people were telling the truth. Darn, who woulda thought!"

"You're crazy like the rest of us," Jimmy said. "Welcome to the Spook Club."

* * *

An ambient moonlight reflected off the Suwannee. Upriver, a ghostly bridge loomed, shadowy and haunting, silhouetted against winking stars in a mysterious heaven.

The boys, mesmerized, continued to gaze at the uncanny manifestation below them.

That's when it happened.

The spring's sandy bottom clouded.

The boys gasped and jerked straight.

The horse bones shuddered, the legs drew up against the rib cage, the head wrenched forward.

Randy mumbled, "I don't believe … what I'm seeing."

Keith, Joe Rea, Ronnie and Jimmy stood droopy mouthed and silent.

The skeleton was gone. The great Gonda stood in the flesh.

Water rushed over the banks onto the boys' feet as the Belgian tried to stand. His head lifted. Muffled neighs shot to the surface. Wild eyes gazed at the frightened boys.

"We've got to help," Jimmy muttered.

The big draft horse reared. His blond mane swam with the current. He lunged. The wagon's hitch swung around, snatching the wheels straight.

The chestnut heaved and lunged. The wagon rocked back and forth.

Jimmy said, "G-gotta d-do some-something."

Ronnie shook his head. "It ain't real."

Gonda's eyes were filled with terror, bubbles escaped his mouth and grunting sounds seeped through the water.

"Gotta help!" Jimmy pushed the boys aside and jumped in. His substantial body transformed into an elegant, graceful swan as he plunged toward Gonda.

"He'll drown," Keith blurted out, and then dove in.

Jimmy already had his hands on the trace lines, trying to unhook the thrashing horse from the wagon hitch. Sand swirled about, making it difficult to see.

Keith kicked toward the bottom.

Gonda lunged, the wagon lurched and Jimmy lost his grip on the trace lines. He was out of air but refused to give up.

But he had to. Bubbles escaped Jimmy's mouth as he exhaled. His body, no longer graceful, floated to the bottom.

Gonda, too, gave up and drifted to the sand. The wagon wheels turned, and once again rested at an angle.

Keith grabbed Jimmy by the arm and kicked toward the surface. But his strength was gone. The remaining air rushed from his lungs.

Ronnie, Joe Rea and Randy splashed into the water, propelling themselves toward their stricken friends. Joe Rea reached Keith first. Wrapping his arm around Keith's waist, he pulled him toward the surface.

Ronnie and Randy caught Jimmy by his arms and lunged upward.

Joe Rea broke the surface first. Keith gulped clean, fresh air into his burning lungs. Then, with Joe Rea's help, he swam to the edge of the spring and crawled out.

Jimmy was limp and unresponsive. Randy felt his pulse. He was still alive.

"Help me sit him up," Randy ordered.

Ronnie slipped his arms underneath Jimmy's shoulders and lifted. Randy straddled Jimmy's body from behind and wrapped his arms around him in a bear hug.

"Hurry," Ronnie pleaded.

Randy pushed his cheek against Jimmy's back and locked his hands around his stomach. He pulled.

Nothing.

He pulled again.

Water spurted from Jimmy's mouth and he gasped for

breath.

“Help me roll him over,” Randy said.

Rolling Jimmy over on his stomach, Randy straddled him and pushed with the palms of his hands into the small of his back.

More water gushed out.

Jimmy sucked in a lung full of fresh summer air, then another, until he was breathing with a steady rhythm.

Keith sat on the bank with his head bowed between his knees, recovering from his near drowning. Joe Rea, out of breath, flopped down beside him.

“You all right, bro?” Ronnie asked.

Jimmy, head cocked to one side, offered a weak smile, then said, “Yeah, I think I’ll live—if you’ll get this doofus off my back.”

Randy hopped to his feet. “I’m glad you’re grateful,” he said with a wide smile.

Jimmy clambered to his feet and gave Randy a bear hug. “Thanks for saving my life,” he said.

“No problem. Think nothing of it.” Randy tapped Jimmy on the shoulder with his fist. “By the way, you’re now my slave!”

“Whew! I’ve gotta pee,” Joe Rea announced, and then did his business.

“Durn!” Jimmy drawled. “I take back what I said about you being a girl.”

* * *

The boys gathered at the edge of the spring. The double-box wagon rested on the bottom and a broken axle lay half submerged in sand beside a wheel turned outward. The bleached bones of the draft horse stretched in front.

The rib cage, the leg bones, the skull with empty eye sockets formed a perfect skeleton. Leather lines black with age, laced through rusty trace rings, stirred with the constant flow of water from the cave.

As the boys watched the ghost wagon and horse bones, the surrounding water began to shimmy and dance in a dreamy manner. Then the ghost wagon and horse bones were gone.

"Look at that," Joe Rea said, pointing toward the surface. "It's a piece of wood."

A gray board bobbled on top of the water. The current caught it, pushing it to the edge of the pool where the boys stood. Then, continuing its journey the wood floated into the winding stream where eventually it joined the tannic waters of the Suwannee.

WEEPING WOMAN WELL

"I'm not getting in that little boat," Jimmy complained. "Besides, it leaks. How are we gonna make it to the other side without sinking?"

"Easy. A bail bucket comes with the boat. Here." Joe Rea handed Jimmy the rusty coffee can. "You're in charge of bailing."

"I'll sing while you bail," Ronnie said, "to keep you in rhythm."

"If you sing, I'll let the boat sink." Jimmy threw the can down. "Drowning will be a more compassionate way of dying."

Four adventurous teens, Keith Dampier, Joe Rea Phillips, Ronnie Miller and Jimmy Redmon stood on the banks of Alligator Lake, one of the largest lakes in Columbia County, Florida. It's also a sinkhole. The great cypress lake, a 350-acre bass fisherman's paradise, can disappear within hours—without warning. Once the sink opens, the whirlpool plunges into the giant hole, leaving only a muddy lake bed and hundreds of rotting fish.

"Okay, men," Keith said with a flip of his head to get the rock-star bangs out of his eyes, "let's turn this thing over and dump the water out."

The old wooden boat, tucked away between a couple cypress trees, wore a faded coat of green paint. Two cracked and weather-worn oars were hidden under it. Nobody knew who owned the boat and no one cared. People used it freely, always putting it back in the same place for the next person, usually a kid who wanted to fish or just have fun on the water.

"I'll hold the boat," Keith said after the boat was pushed into the water. "Everybody get in, then I'll push off."

Jimmy, the first to board the rickety boat, lowered his substantial body into the stern. The boat sank low in the water.

"Geez," Joe Rea griped, "we don't have to worry about the boat leaking. Biggie will sink it by himself."

"I'll gladly stay behind," Jimmy shot back. "Besides, I don't like the idea of walking through those Indian burial mounds. It's creepy."

With everyone in the boat, Keith gave it a shove, jumping into its bow as it glided away. Ronnie and Joe Rea, grabbing the paddles, swished the bow around to face the opposite shore.

"Yeee-hi! Here goes the Five Points Spook Club off to solve another mystery!" Ronnie announced.

"Yeah, sure, or die trying!" Jimmy knew how to spread the sarcasm honey thick.

Jimmy had little enthusiasm for his friends' never-ending adventures—and for good reasons.

Keith, Joe Rea, Ronnie and Jimmy loosely called themselves the Five Points Spook Club after accidently falling into their first adventure while exploring an abandoned railroad track. All of them lived in North Florida, in a neighborhood called Five Points, located two miles north of Lake City.

The boys had escaped death by a phantom train; outlived an otherworldly encounter in a haunted house; gotten out of the grips of a demon-eyed beast and survived two near-drownings in Branford Springs while trying to save a ghost horse. Jimmy had no reason to believe their latest adventure would be any less threatening.

Joe Rea gazed at the threatening clouds. "Look at that sky. Looks like we're in for it."

"Great! Not only does the boat leak," Jimmy said as he dumped water overboard, "but we—uh, I—have to bail out rainwater as well."

"You're doing a good job, Biggie," Keith ragged. "Keep up the good work!"

"Yeah, while you sit and watch, right?"

"Hey, somebody has to navigate."

Thunder rolled through the dark gray belly of clouds, grumbling like a hungry giant. A splattering of rain began to fall.

"There, see? What did I tell you," Jimmy wailed. "It's a frog strangler."

Keith rolled his eyes. "It's only a sprinkle, Redmon, for chrissakes! Besides, you won't melt."

"No, but I might die of pneumonia, strep throat, the Black Plague—or something really serious—like dandruff."

Everyone chuckled.

The four sailors rowed past cypress trees standing like islands throughout the lake. A bull gator grunted. A fish jumped. An egret stood in a slough covered in bald cypress knees.

They were halfway across when Joe Rea asked, "So, Dampier, who told you about this haunted well?"

"Bobby."

"Bobby?" Jimmy groaned. "Ah, nuts!"

Ronnie snapped, "That's what you need to hang with *us*."

"Or have no brains," Jimmy chimed in. "That should qualify you to be president of this stupid Spook Club!"

Bobby wasn't a name Jimmy wanted to hear. Bobby, Keith's neighbor, had been the one responsible for telling them about the glowing house in the woods, which turned out to be haunted.

"You can count on Bobby," said Joe Rea.

"Yeah," Jimmy agreed, "to lead us into danger."

"While you're busy navigating," Ronnie said to Keith, "why don't you give us the low-down about this Weeping Woman Well?"

"You remember from your Florida history in school the story about Chief Alligator … I forget his Seminole name …"

"Halpatter Tuskenuggee," Joe Rea said. "Sorry …"

"Don't stop," Keith encouraged him. "You're the brain, you can tell it better than I can."

"Tuskenuggee settled along the banks of this lake—"

"That's why it's called Lake Alligator," Jimmy said, proud of his knowledge.

"You're a freakin' genius!" Joe Rea mocked.

"Smart-ass!" Jimmy fired back.

"May I?"

"Be my guest."

Joe Rea cleared his throat. "A white settlement that sprang up near the Seminole village in the 1830s was called Alligator Town, after the old chief. In 1856 the town was renamed—"

"Lake City!"

Joe Rea glared at Jimmy and said, "You should be on *Jeopardy*!"

"Shove it!"

Keith, sitting in the bow of the boat, intervened. "Knock it off, you two. You've had the history lesson from the genius and his minion. Now let me educate you about the legend of Weeping Woman Well. In the 1830s until after the Civil War, runaway slaves joined the Seminoles for protection. In turn, the slaves fought beside them during the Seminole Wars. Some of the slaves lived right in the village while others established homesteads close by.

"One slave by the name of Noah Elijah built himself a cabin on the other side of this lake, past the burial mounds. He had a wife named Sally and they had a son, named Joshua. Well, one day Joshua went to the village, leaving his wife and four-year-old child behind."

"Go ahead," Jimmy said, "get to the part where we put our lives in danger."

"Hey, would I do that?"

"Do skunks smell?"

"Have a little faith. Bobby hasn't led us wrong yet."

"Oh, geez," Jimmy groaned, and bailed another bucketful.

The rain came down a little harder.

"As I was saying … Sally got busy doing chores or something, when she heard a splash. The baby had wandered out to the well and fallen in."

"That's terrible," Ronnie said. "So she got him out, right?"

"That's the bad part. The baby cried and begged his mother for help. She tried to get him out, but couldn't."

"I hate sad stories like that," Joe Rea whined.

"Wanna know what else?" Keith gazed at his rapt audience. "The baby could have been saved. Two men rode by on horseback. When Sally pleaded for help, they laughed and said, 'One less darky in the world.' They rode off, with Sally running behind, begging them to save her baby. Joshua drowned, calling his mama for help."

"Hey look, Biggie's crying," Ronnie said.

"I am not! Splashed water in my eye, that's all."

Joe Rea quickly wiped a tear with his shirtsleeve.

"The legend goes, Sally mourned herself to death kneeling by the well. They say you can still hear her weeping on—and get this—rainy days."

"That explains why you wanted to wait until it rained," Joe Rea said.

Jimmy groaned.

"Oh, one more thing …"

The boat's V-hull sliced into the mud on the shore.

* * *

Keith, Joe Rea, Jimmy and Ronnie pulled the boat onto shore into a grove of cypress. Then the bottom fell out.

"Like, we're totally crazy?" Ronnie remarked.

"Thank you," Jimmy said. "That confirms it, you're the president."

"Which way?" Joe Rea asked.

"According to Bobby, we follow the lake past the Indian mounds, to that thicket of pine." Keith pointed to the trees.

They squinted against the heavy rain that obscured their vision.

"Around that thicket stands a huge oak tree," Keith said. "The cabin was there."

Tin rattled across the sky and the downpour continued. Rain, stinging their faces, forced them to walk with heads down, Alice in Chains hair plastered to scalps. Clothes clung like glue to their skin. The drowning rats turned from the lake, stumbling toward the pine thicket. After a hard trek across fields of wiry grass and mud they spotted the Seminole graveyard.

"There they are," Keith said. "The burial mounds."

Jimmy, walking on the side facing the mounds, scooted to the opposite side. "Just in case," he said.

* * *

The teenage sleuths stood at the entrance of the pine thicket, and the rain finally slacked off to a moderate drizzle.

Keith said, "That looks like smoke."

Above the treetops, through drizzle and dreary light, a wispy snake of smoke faded into matching gray sky. The boys looked at each other. No houses were supposed to be on this land. Protected by the state of Florida to preserve the nearby burial grounds, this property was to remain pristine. Knowing this, the four adventure hunters were perplexed.

Joe Rea said, "I think we've stumbled onto someone's house."

"Oh, great! Now we're gonna get shot," Jimmy said. "Why worry about pneumonia when I can die by shotgun?"

"May as well check it out while we're here," Ronnie said, stepping into the pine grove.

"Let's all follow President Crazy," Jimmy smart-mouthed.

Then they heard it.

Wailing, splashing, coughing, gurgling.

They peeked through the trees.

Standing by a giant live oak sat a log cabin of rough-hewed pine logs. Smoke curled from a stone chimney.

Heart-wrenching sobs passed through the rain-soaked air, followed by a wailing cry: "My baby! My baby!"

"Mama, Mama, help me," came a small begging voice, barely audible.

"Somebody needs help," Ronnie shouted. "Come on, let's go!"

Ronnie, Keith and Joe Rea scrambled for the cabin. Jimmy lumbered behind.

The voices became louder as they approached.

"Somebody help me!" she screamed. "Oh Lawd, save my baby." The woman's agonizing screams turned to whimpering pleas.

"Mama, Mama." The small voice, interrupted by gasping coughs, became weaker.

Ronnie rounded the cabin.

The woman turned.

He slid to a stop. Stared.

"What the—" His heart leapt.

Keith and Joe Rea slammed into each other trying to stop.

The woman ran toward the boys, arms stretched, tears flowing. "Please! Save my baby, Masa, he be drownin' in the well! Oh, please!"

Surprised, the boys leapt backward.

Jimmy plodded to a stop.

A young black woman wearing a loose-fitting sack dress, hair bundled Aunt Jemima–style, fell at their feet.

"Please, Masa," she wailed, "my baby be drownin'."

She grabbed Ronnie's legs and he fell backward onto the muddy ground.

The voice in the well faded. Only coughs and gurgles reached the stone opening.

Jimmy, ignoring the woman, rushed to the well.

The former slave, seeing Jimmy, ran back to the well.

Jimmy peered into the well, looking for the source of the cries.

The child went under.

Recovering from the shock, Ronnie, Keith and Joe Rea scrambled to join Jimmy.

"I'm going in," Jimmy shouted. He started to climb over the stone wall.

"Wait!" Ronnie pulled him back. "Let me."

The boy's head popped out of the water, arms thrashing.

Ronnie jumped, landing beside the drowning child. He grabbed him with one arm and treaded water with the other.

"Untie the bucket," Ronnie yelled. "Send the rope down."

The knot was too tight. Keith flicked out his Kershaw and sliced the rope.

Joe Rea grabbed the handle and turned counterclockwise. With a squeak, the rope descended into the well.

"It's okay ...." Ronnie looked up and asked, "What's your son's name, ma'am?"

"It be Joshua."

"It's okay, Joshua. We'll get you outta here."

Joshua smiled as his tears dried up.

"Pull," Ronnie ordered. "Easy!"

With the rope secured around Joshua's chest just under his arms, they pulled the boy to safety.

The mother took him into her arms, held him close and wept.

With the rope back in the well, Ronnie tied it around himself.

"Outta the way, boys," Jimmy said, beaming a smile. "Let a man in here."

Jimmy grabbed the rope and pulled. Ronnie stretched, putting his feet on the stone casing, and started walking up the side. Keith and Joe Rea held on to a piece of the rope, leaning back as they helped pull.

Ronnie tumbled over the rock wall, landing on the ground. His three friends collapsed beside him.

"Thank you," a grateful voice said.

The boys looked.

The woman with the child in her arms beamed a lovely smile … and they faded away.

Where the cabin had stood a minute earlier, wildflowers now swayed in the breeze, soaking up the summer rain. Chunks of blackened chimney lay scattered among the flowers. Part of the well's rock shell still existed—crumbled. Someone had placed green treated boards over the shaft to prevent anyone from falling in.

"Well, I'll be darned!" Keith pointed to something lying a few feet from the well. A wooden bucket, the bottom rotted out, lay sideways in the weeds.

Jimmy smiled and said, "I wouldn't have believed *anything* that just happened if I had been with anyone besides you crazy people."

Keith laughed and said, "It's an exclusive club, bro."

Everyone high-fived.

* * *

The afternoon sky still dropped rain, but the boys didn't mind. They passed through the pine grove, heading toward the boat.

"By the way," Joe Rea said, remembering the 'one more thing' Keith had mentioned, "what was, as Paul Harvey says, *the rest of the story*?"

"I didn't tell you?"

They waited.

"Because of hatred and prejudice, Joshua drowned. The legend goes … if someone showed love and compassion toward Sally by trying to save Joshua, then the boy would have lived and his mother wouldn't have mourned herself to death."

"Who would've thunk it," Ronnie said. "Me, a hero!"

The boys approached the burial mounds. Standing on top were three silent figures: a man, a woman, and in her arms, a boy. They smiled and waved.

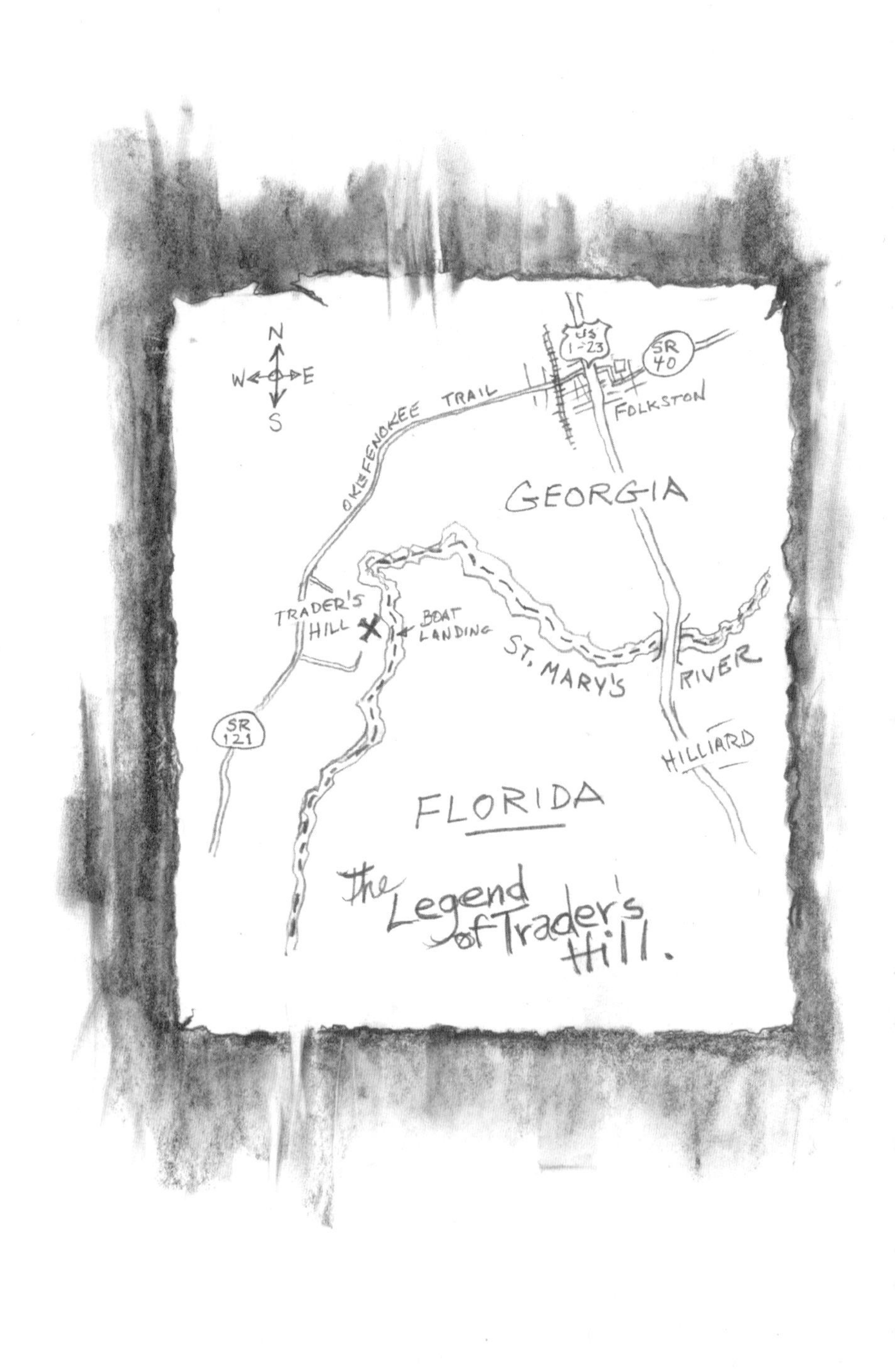
N
W
E
S
US
1-23
SR
40
OKEFENOKEE TRAIL
FOLKSTON
GEORGIA
TRADER'S
HILL
BOAT
LANDING
ST. MARY'S
RIVER
SR
121
HILLIARD
FLORIDA
The Legend of Trader's Hill.

THE LEGENDS OF TRADERS HILL

Traders Hill, located in southeast Georgia on the St. Marys River, started off as a trading post. It became a major commerce center for river trade and eventually developed into a town. By 1854 a two-story log courthouse had been built and Traders Hill became the county seat.

The town thrived until the Savannah, Florida & Western Railroad was built a little farther north. The log courthouse burnt for the second time and the seat of government was moved to Folkston. By 1901 the town was gone.

"The Secret of Traders Hill" and "The Witch of Traders Hill" are eerie stories that have been told and retold over the years. When the town died, something else died with it … a dark secret, an unthinkable evil.

Like all secrets, however, in time they are exposed.

THE SECRET OF TRADERS HILL

"This should be a good area to set up a tree stand," Danny observed.

"It looks promising," Colt agreed. "Plenty of deer tracks around here."

Danny and Colt, high school seniors and passionate hunters, were on a scouting expedition in the forest surrounding the abandoned Traders Hill community. The sweet scent of pine needles, sap and wildflowers mingled for the unmistakable smell of the waning days of summer. Palmettos rattled like dry bones as the two friends pushed their way through thick undergrowth.

"Hey Danny, remember the stories about the old Brewster place?"

"Yeah, I heard Dad and his friends talk about it at the hunting club." Danny stepped over a dead-fall and paused. "The cabin, or what's left of it, should be around in this area."

"Nobody has been through these woods for years," Colt said. "The former owners wouldn't let anybody back here to hunt, look around or anything. Man, wouldn't it be crazy if we found it?"

"Yeah, that would be awesome. I heard the men at camp talk about old Brewster. He was a real scoundrel. The people of Traders Hill suspected him of murder, but they could never prove it. So everybody sorta shunned him, made him an outcast." Spider-legged shivers ran down Danny's spine.

Colt spotted more deer tracks. "Looks like a big buck lives around here. We had better get busy and scout this place out before dark."

Staying alert for rattlesnakes, they pushed through palmettos. Chattering squirrels dashed up trees when the boys approached.

"Hey, look at that." Colt pointed to a lone magnolia tree several yards away. Its large fragrant white flowers bloomed stark and stunning against the yellow pines surrounding it. "Strange sight for the middle of a pine forest, don't you think? Come on, bro, let's check it out."

"Yeah, that is crazy."

They made their way through thickets of grasping palmettos and gallberry bushes, toward the lone magnolia. Getting closer, they noticed something gray and cracked jutting from the tall weeds.

"Would you look at that? It's a fence post." Danny walked around the magnolia to get a close-up look. "Daaamn! I believe we've found it!"

"Yep, sure as heck. And look at that, it's a fence. How cool is that?"

The post, gray and cracked from years of relentless sun and rain, held remnants of a split-rail fence. Rotted logs half eaten by insects and worms lay scattered about.

"Man, this is spooky," Danny said, and shivered again.

"Creepy!"

"Eerie!"

"Menacing!"

"Weird!"

"Yeah, like you," Colt teased.

"Thank you."

"Don't mention it."

Then Colt spotted something else around a stand of scrubby blackjack. "Well, I'll be … it's a chimney!"

The remains of a chimney with pitted mortar covered with green algae stood as a stark reminder of the past. It leaned to one side in its final days of collapse. The boys walked closer and upon further inspection found it still connected to a blackened fireplace.

Danny let out a low whistle. "Awesome, we've actually found it!"

Like a sudden change in seasons, a cold, gripping fear stabbed them in the back. Pure terror invaded every nerve and thread of their strong bodies.

The boys had a powerful urge to turn around.

But they dared not.

Knife-sharp instincts strongly revealed that something or someone was watching. Anxiously, Danny and Colt turned to face each other, their live-wire nerves twitching.

Something frightening stood behind them.

They jerked around, gasping at the sight.

"Darn!" Colt stumbled backward and fell.

Danny shuddered. His heart sprinted.

Three young girls stood side by side, staring, faces drawn and haunting. Sunken, unblinking coal-black eyes were completely void of light. Ashen skin shrouded frail bodies. Blonde hair braided into pigtails touched their shoulders. Without saying a word, the three girls turned as one and then moved toward the river.

The mind-fog finally lifting from Danny's brain, he said, "What the …"

"Heck was that!" Colt finished, leaping to his feet.

"Hey, little girls," Danny shouted, "what are you doing out here?"

No answer came, nor did the girls look back. Loose-fitting ankle-length white dresses, faded to a dirty yellow, covered their slight bodies. Drawstrings on the backs of the dresses held them closed.

Colt asked, "Dude, what the heck was that?"

"Heck if I know, but something sure is strange about those girls. And did you notice they're barefoot—out here in the woods with briers and rattlesnakes, for chrissakes."

The girls moved single file with ease through thick brush and razor-sharp palmettos, seemingly without a scratch. Their long dresses flowed without a pull or snag.

"Makes no freakin' sense, youngins alone out here in the middle of the freakin' woods." Colt's voice expressed apprehension and concern.

"Come on, let's follow them," Danny said, stepping over a pile of algae-covered bricks.

Without slowing, the three girls breezed along stirring nothing … not a bush or a twig nor did dry leaves and pine needles crunch underneath their feet.

A whip-poor-will called and its mate answered.

A storm of flapping wings erupted from nearby trees. Cardinals, with blazing red vestments and black masks, swooped from trees, flying directly over the girls. The loud, clear whistles echoed each other.

Then an army of blue jays, feathers a vivid lavender-blue, appeared from the sky. Jayer, jayer, they called, darting to and fro like arrows.

Startled, Colt and Danny froze in their tracks.

"Dude," Danny said, his voice strained, "this is getting weirder by the second."

"Durn straight it is!"

"This is really starting to freak me out." With worried eyes Danny watched the army of birds hover over the girls.

The three girls stopped, turned and faced the perplexed teenagers. Not a word was uttered. A cloud of red, gray and blue swooned overhead, forming a cardinal–blue jay halo.

Suddenly a loud caul, caul, echoed from the deep woods. The haunting cauls became more and more distinct as the seconds passed. Then, with a noisy flutter, two crows with black gloss-violet feathers plunged from high in the air, joining the other birds.

Colt and Danny remained steadfast in their tracks, reluctant to go on.

The two magpies whirled, then shot toward the two boys.

Danny exclaimed, "Oh crap!" and threw up an arm shield.

Colt hit the ground.

Harsh cauls resounded from agitated crows as they dive-bombed past anxious boys. Then, after a couple of passes, the two friends realized what the birds were doing.

"I guess they're waiting on us," Danny said, stepping forward. He wiped sweaty palms on the pockets of his Wranglers.

Colt stood brushing off clinging pine straw from his faded jeans. "Well, I'll just be darned!" he said, shaking his head in disbelief while stepping behind Danny like a soldier on the march.

The waiting girls turned immediately, continuing their effortless trek through the bushes. Chattering cardinals and jays made an arched turn, resuming their protective flight over the girls. The crows joined them.

"Unless I've lost my mind, and I'm saying that's highly possibly at this point, I believe the birds are escorting those girls," Colt observed once he caught up with Danny.

"I think you're right, buddy."

They continued to follow, this time at a steady trot.

"Hey girls, wait up," Danny called again, this time in a gentler voice, trying not to alarm them. "Hold up a minute while we catch up."

But they didn't stop or look back; the mysterious moppets kept moving like the invisible air around them.

"Have you noticed something?" Danny asked through heavy breaths. "No matter how fast we go, those youngins manage to stay ahead of us. We can't seem to get any closer."

"How can I not notice? The youngest can't be more than six years old and the oldest more than ten, but they still stay ahead of us. Something's seriously wrong with this picture."

The girls, stepping from forest shadows, glimpsed the river. Their cheerless faces grew even sadder. High banks were lined with regal pine and moss-draped oaks gnarled with a century of age. Their roots, snaking down the bluff toward the water, weaved in and out of the soil. Dark water flowed languidly, rippling over a half submerged log with one end buried in mud at water's edge.

The three girls walked to the periphery of the bluff and then stopped. The youngest child hugged a doll to her chest. Its body was made of coarse burlap cloth and its head of carved wood with a painted face. The doll's hair consisted of corn shuck, brown and dry. Its head rested against the young girl's sad cheek.

Danny and Colt, approaching the river, slowed their pace. The three girls, standing firm, stared at the tepid water below.

The boys eased closer.

Jays and cardinals, fluttering near the treetops, circled in a holding pattern. The crows lighted on an oak limb, each giving out a harsh caul, caul!

The three youngsters stood side by side like a wall, intent on the passing river below them. Loose hair around their braids wisped with the sultry but gentle breeze. With fluid motion, they raised their heads and slowly turned, facing the boys, who now stood within arm's length of them.

Blank eyes penetrated the teenagers' souls.

"Lord, have mercy!" Colt jumped backward, tripping over an exposed tree root.

"Oh, geez!" Danny shuddered and grasped the bib of his cap.

The haunting spectacle of sightless eyes shot chills of terror through the boys.

The girls did not move.

As if waking from a daze, in a slow drawl Danny asked, "What is it? What are you trying to tell us?" He adjusted his cap, waiting for an answer.

Without a word all three girls turned and pointed toward the river.

A brisk wind rattled through the trees.

Then the air was still again. Together, the girls turned and walked into the brush. The bird halo followed.

Colt and Danny, not knowing what to do, stood and stared

after the youngsters.

Caul! Caul! The crows sprang from the oak limb with a fluttering ruckus and whizzed by too close past the startled boys. Flinching, Danny and Colt shielded their heads. The crows turned and conducted one more dive before joining the menagerie of cardinals and blue jays.

Danny, taking the hint, adjusted his cap again, saying matter-of-factly, “Well, bro, we’d better get moving before we get our eyes pecked out.”

“I guess we’d darn well better,” Colt agreed, pushing up from the dusty ground and brushing himself off.

The girls, satisfied their followers had gotten the message, turned onto a winding game trail that pulled them deeper into the forest. After pursuing the narrow trail for some time the strange girls veered into the underbrush.

Danny and Colt followed, painstakingly pushing their way through brush, vine fortresses, biting briers and around trees. Their arms and hands bled, their clothes snagged and ripped from the saw-like palmettos and clinging briers. The girls still were unaffected, and glided unbridled through the maze of vegetation. The followers were close behind but, as before and despite their efforts, could not catch up.

“This is crazy,” Colt said through labored breaths. “They want to show us something, but what?”

“I don’t understand and I know this is crazy, but I don’t feel threatened. Scared as heck, yes, but not threatened.”

The girls were gone.

“We’ve lost them!” Colt said hastily, looking around. His searching eyes caught a glimpse of something bright and colorful. “Look, there, through the trees!”

“Awesome!” Danny said, catching sight of vibrant colors around a colonnade of trees. “C’mon,” he said with a wave of the hand. “We’ve got to check this out.”

The boys broke through a barrier of pine and stumbled into a field of unimaginable beauty. A furtive garden of honeysuckle, dainty blue forget-me-not, white primrose with yellow eyes, mixed iris, blue, yellow and violet, formed a garland rainbow. Succulent air dripped with delight. The boys, amazed at the sight, stood and gawked.

"Geez, would you look at that?" Colt said, and trilled a low whistle. "A flower garden in the middle of these scrubby woods!"

"Totally awesome!"

Jayer, jayer, came rapid calls from the blue jays.

Robust crimson plumage of the male cardinals fluffed down on proud heads as the birds trilled, cheer-cheer-cheer-what-what-what, sharply and clearly. Together they circled over the girls, and then in one giant swing, vanished over the canopy of green pine.

The three girls stood, waiting in the center of the garden, staring intently at Colt and Danny, who were still gazing at the bird-less sky.

The impatient crows again dive-bombed behind the mesmerized boys, who felt the wind from wildly flapping wings. Talons touched shoulders. Startled, the boys recoiled and hunched over, throwing their arms up for protection. The frenzied magpies shot over their heads like arrows and swooshed toward the waiting girls. Then they too were gone.

Colt and Danny looked at each other with stark amazement.

"They're waiting," Colt said, wading into the flowers. "Come on, let's go and see what they have to show us."

The teenagers walked within arm's length of the girls, who stood patiently and unblinking. The youngest girl sadly touched her cheek to the tattered doll.

With stretched-out arms and pointing fingers the girls beckoned toward the ground. Slowly Colt and Danny turned their gaze toward the earth. There, in front of them, the outline of three sunken graves lay beneath the wildflowers.

"Graves," Danny whispered. He looked at the girls.

Tears seeped from their eyes, falling to the sunken ground beneath bare feet. Their hopeless expressions were unforgettable as they pleaded for understanding.

Colt understood. “Those are your graves, aren’t they, girls?”

Then Danny knew. “Old Brewster drowned you in the river and buried you here, didn’t he?”

The children nodded, smiling for the first time. Their eyes, once dead, now glowed with a heavenly radiance.

Satisfied at last, they yielded to slanting rays of sunlight as its warmth penetrated their bodies. They became fainter and fainter until only glowing faces remained visible. Then, with misty smiles they vanished, happy that the secret of Traders Hill was at long last revealed.

WELCO
TRADE

THE WITCH OF TRADERS HILL

"I don't like the idea of this ghost town and witch business," Samantha complained.

"Come on, Sam, lighten up, it'll be fun." Doug leaned over and kissed his girlfriend on the cheek. Her pouty mouth instantly turned up into a smile. "Besides," he added, "I'll protect you from the old witch."

Samantha's green eyes sparkled. "You'd better," she said, giving him a playful shove.

"What about you, Charlie. You gonna protect me from the evil old witch?" Valerie smiled and snuggled up to Charlie's tall athletic frame. Her long blonde hair fluttered in the breeze as the boat hurried upriver.

"Are you kidding?" A sly smile crossed Charlie's Superman face. "Doug's the hero here, not me. He'll protect you." Valerie slid away.

"Hey, chill out, I was just teasing. You know I will."

"You'd better say that, Charlie Wood, or I'll find me a new boyfriend, one that *will* protect me." Valerie smiled, sliding back to her snuggle position.

The Evinrude purred, plowing toward Traders Hill.

"So, what happened to the town?" Val asked.

"It sorta disappeared around the turn of the twentieth century when the railroad bypassed it. Of course, the real reason it vanished," said Doug with a sly look, "is because Hattie Jenkins put a curse on the town … just before they executed her." Doug smiled. He had their attention.

"That's creepy!" Valerie shivered, pressing closer to Charlie.

"And that's not all," Doug continued. "Three young girls disappeared—just vanished one day. Nobody ever found them. They claimed it was on account of the curse. In fact, a lot of people went missing after she put *the evil eye* on the town."

"Oh, pul-eeze," Sam scoffed. "You don't seriously believe that stuff, do you?"

"Why not?" Doug said with a wave of his hand. "A lot of strange things happened after they killed Hattie. And after all, the town is gone."

"So, why did they kill the poor old woman?" Val asked.

"She killed her husband," Doug said flatly. "Old Hoag Jenkins used her as a punching bag. He even beat her with a piece of firewood when she accidently knocked over a jug of moonshine."

"Huh! Sounds like he deserved it, if you ask me," Val said curtly.

"Wanna know how she killed the old man?" Doug knew he could make the girls squirm. "She chopped his head off!"

Sam recoiled, saying, "Ee-yoo, that's so gross!"

"Anyway," Doug went on, "the whole town turned out to watch her hang and not one person came to her defense."

Val said, "They should have given her a medal."

"They did, sort of." Doug chuckled. "They gave her a metal—ax."

"Ee-yoo!" Sam said again.

"They tried to hang her, but before the hangman could spring the trap door, a mob rushed the gallows and dragged her away. The town cheered them on. They took her to the rear of the courthouse, tied her hands behind her back and stretched her neck over a tree stump." Doug stopped for effect.

"Well?" Charlie prodded. "You gonna tell us or not?"

Doug throttled the Evinrude back to idle, letting the boat drift.

"They had her on the chopping block ready to swing the

ax when she lifted her head and looked at the crowd." Doug leaned forward before continuing. "The mob went silent. Not a word was said. Old Hattie continued to study the people. As she watched, a slow grin crossed her wrinkled face. Her eyes, they say, had the glint of a cat. Evil eye, they called it." Doug's hands were animated. " 'You'll all pay for this,' she hissed. 'You'll see. The whole town will pay!' The townspeople, turned mob, shouted, 'Witch! Witch!' over and over again—"

"Maybe they should have named the town Salem," Charlie said, smiling.

"Uh-huh." Doug cleared his throat. "To finish the story, it took three chops with a dull ax before her head rolled to the sand."

"You're making that up," Val said.

"Maybe old Hattie did put a curse on the town." Doug's expression had turned thoughtful. "I didn't pay much attention at the time, but I do remember the men at the hunting club talking about Traders Hill and all the mysterious things that happened there."

"Like what?" Sam asked.

"The church caught fire … while the preacher gave his sermon. The courthouse burnt twice. People sorta disappeared, like the three girls, and were never heard from again. The ones responsible for executing Hattie all came to a bad end."

Charlie asked, "What happened to the town?"

"The railroad came along. River trade stopped, and the town sort of faded away. Then, to seal its fate," Doug said, "a tornado ripped through the town, destroying every last building."

"That don't mean it was Hattie's curse that caused it," Sam said curtly. "You can't believe everything you hear. Besides, there's no such thing as a witch."

"Oh yes there is too," Charlie said. "Old lady Snedaker, from chemistry class."

"See there?" Doug laughed. "What more proof do you need?"

The boat was drifting toward shore. Grabbing the wheel, Doug eased the throttle forward. The small craft swooshed in the direction of Traders Hill.

A blue heron standing at water's edge cautiously watched the boat pass. Oak trees, old and regal, posed like sentinels stretching over the ancient river, with their gray mossy beards dangling. Light from a golden sun streaked through the pine forest and palmetto fields. A cloudless blue sky sheltered the earth like a blanket. The sunny and glorious day seemed right for an adventure, but Doug Eubanks, Samantha Richards, Charlie Wood and Valerie Morgan, mesmerized by the beauty of nature and blinded by the innocence of youth, could not foretell the dangers lurking in the ruins of Traders Hill.

"We're almost there," Doug said, pointing out the decaying bulkhead. "That's the landing at Traders Hill."

As soon as Val saw it, even from a distance, her spirit slumped. An involuntary shiver sent goose bumps tingling through her. "Oh, I don't like it here," Val cried. "It feels *so* wrong. I think we should go back."

"Aw, come on, Val," Doug whined. "You can't be serious. What's wrong about it?"

"I don't know, it just feels creepy, that's all."

"It does feel strange," Sam agreed. "Maybe she's right."

"Don't tell me you two are going all girly on us," Charlie said with a chuckle.

"Like, yes," Val shot back. "And why not, we *are* girls." Her shoulder-length blonde hair fluttered in the wind as the boat droned its way toward the landing.

Charlie's brown eyes, despite Doug's enthusiasm, showed a hint of concern when they approached the shore. The river outing had seemed like a good idea. The excitement of doing something new, especially with the girls, had the promise of an affable day. Now Charlie had doubts.

Doug, on the other hand, seemed unconcerned. A wide smile punctuated the dimples at the corners of his mouth. It was an adventure for him, a harmless jaunt up the river, a fun excursion into a storied piece of history filled with innocuous legends. He had no reason to worry.

Doug cut the engine, allowing the boat to glide toward shore. The sharp bow sliced into the mud, which brought the small craft to a halt on the edge of the bank.

"This is it," Doug said, sweeping a wide swath with his arm. "Traders Hill, home of the evil witch." Doug pushed off the bow with his right hand and sailed over the side. He sank to his ankles. "Oh crap!" he said.

Charlie scowled and said, "Bummer, dude. You landed us in a mud bog." He eased himself off the boat and into the mire.

"E-yoo," Valerie protested. "Like, you don't expect me to put my new shoes in that, do you?"

"Hey, society girl," Charlie said, "I told you not to wear your good stuff out here in the boonies."

"Like, you don't expect me to go out in public looking like a back woods hick, do you?"

"Like, yes. Look around you. What do you see?" Charlie turned his back to the boat and extended his arms. "Climb on, society girl, I'll save your pretty shoes."

"And what about me?" Sam asked, staring at her boyfriend. Doug wasn't paying attention. "Like, Doug?"

"Oh, uh, sorry," Doug said, sloshing back through the mud.

A graveyard of barnacle-encrusted pilings jutted from the water, a ghostly reminder of the town's heyday when busy docks were piled high with lumber and other trading goods. The remains of a protective bulkhead still lined the bank, most of it intact. The remnants of a dock jutted lengthwise of the river for several yards.

"Ol' Hattie won't care what you're wearing anyhow," Doug said with a grin. "She won't be interested in fashion, just your head."

"My head?" Sam asked.

Throwing Charlie a wink, Doug said, "Sure, you know how the legend goes, right?"

Charlie took the hint. "Hattie takes revenge on anybody dumb enough to step foot on this land … that would be us."

Valerie rolled her eyes. "Yeah, right!"

"It's true." Doug looked serious. "Hattie swore she would chop off the heads of anybody stepping foot on this very land."

"Na-uh." Sam's face skewed into a grimace. "You're just making that up to scare us."

"Scout's honor," Doug said, giving the two-finger honor sign. "It's the truth."

"He's right," Charlie said. "But remember, it's only a legend." He nodded at Doug, "Finish the story, bro."

"Well," Doug continued, "Ol' Hattie walks around carrying her head in one hand and an ax in the other, waiting for her next victim."

"Get real," Val said.

"Uh-huh, it's true," Charlie said, taking over for Doug. "Hattie drags her victim to the chopping block and cuts his head off. Then," he added, "She takes the head and places it in her grave."

"And the graveyard is still here," Doug jumped in. "It's in the back of the church, or at least where the church used to be. All that's left now are the cement steps."

A chilly wind blew in from the river.

"Oh," Valerie said, hugging herself, "something just happened."

"Like, she's right," Sam said, her eyes shifting slowly. "Something did happen, I could feel it."

"Dude," Charlie said slowly, "I felt it too!"

"Get real," Doug said, "it's just your imagination working overtime."

But Doug, too, had felt it. He tried to push the eerie feeling aside. After all, he was just having fun; it wasn't real.

A shiver gave him the heebie-jeebies. *Get a grip,* he told himself. He tried to shake it, but the feeling persisted.

"I think we should go," Val said, and pulled on Charlie's arm. "Come on, let's get out of this creepy place."

Charlie said, "Dude, come on."

Doug refused to admit something was wrong. "We were only kidding. Where's your sense of adventure?"

"This is really, really freaking me out," Sam said. "I'm with Val. We should go."

"Maybe they're right," Charlie said.

"Aw, come on, Charlie," Doug said, "not you too?" Then he brightened up. "Hey, I got it," he said, wiggling his eyebrows. "We can make out in the cemetery. Wouldn't *that* be cool?"

Charlie perked up. "Yeah, cool," he said, leaning to kiss Val on the lips.

Val quickly turned her head. "I suggest you and Doug make out with Hattie!"

"I think Doug would rather make out with Hattie, anyway," Sam remarked with a hint of sarcasm.

"Not true," Doug countered. "She's hot, but not as hot as you, babe." He put his arms over Sam's shoulders and kissed her gently.

"Ohhh, how sweet," Valerie mocked.

Sam sighed, revealing soft dimples. "Okay, you win. But if I'm going to donate my head to old Hattie, I may as well look good." She dug a tube of lipstick out of her jeans and screwed it open.

"Cool, now you're talking!" Doug's adventurous spirit returned. He pointed and said, "I think the graveyard is that-a-way. Come on, let's go."

The mood lightened as they walked where the town once stood. Pieces of rotted lumber lay scattered, left where the tornado had dropped them. Rock and cement supports stood as tombstones marking the life and death of grand houses and humble cabins.

"According to an old map of Traders Hill I pulled up on

the Internet, the church stood on the outskirts of town, but, like I said, only the cement steps are left." He dug the map out of his back pocket and unfolded it. "The graveyard is here," he said, pointing to a symbol on the map representing a cemetery. "Hattie's buried in an unmarked grave way in the back, separate from the other graves."

"This is getting creepy," Valerie said. "Do you think Hattie's ghost could really be there?"

"Val," Sam said, rolling her eyes, "get real."

"That's what we're gonna find out in just a few minutes," Doug said.

"I wouldn't count on seeing a ghost if I were you," Charlie said with a chuckle.

"But it's possible, right?" Val asked, not knowing what to believe.

"Hey," Doug said, "anything's possible. Personally, I believe ghosts do exist, or at least spirits, in some form or another."

"I guess you have a point," Charlie agreed. "After all, the devil is a spirit."

"Stop it!" Val said, not liking the tone of the conversation. "I think we're asking for trouble when we talk like that. We shouldn't mention, like, you know, the devil and all that stuff."

Then Sam noticed her long shadow. "Hey, you guys, it's getting late. We'd better head for home before it gets dark."

"We've got plenty of time," Doug said. He motioned toward the sun. "At least another two hours."

Doug had deliberately arrived at Traders Hill late in the afternoon so the sun would be low on the horizon. He wanted shadows from the trees and tombstones and everything the warm, slanted rays touched, to elongate into mysterious effigies of lurking creatures for the ultimate effect.

"I think we're in the middle of town," Doug said. "The map shows the courthouse once stood right about there." He pointed toward the spot.

"Awesome!" Charlie said. "Part of the back wall is still standing. How cool is that?"

They walked over and stared at the blackened logs.

"It's creepy," Val said. She shuddered, hugging her arms to herself.

In a low, whispery voice, Sam asked, "So, the chopping block should be here too, right?"

"It's marked right here, see?" Doug pointed to an ax symbol marking the execution spot. "If the map is correct, it should be right behind that wall."

Sam, Charlie, Val and even Doug felt apprehensive about actually seeing the spot where the witch of Traders Hill had been executed. They walked slowly through tall weeds and clumps of palmettos covering the area.

Charlie tripped. "Oh, my leg!"

Val rushed to help. "Are you hurt?"

Pulling himself into a sitting position, he rocked back and forth. "Man, it hurts!" Blood trickled down his leg.

All three gathered around Charlie.

"Hey, dude, are you hurt?" Doug asked.

Charlie slowly pulled up his torn pant leg, scared at what he might see. Blood oozed from a cut. "Durn it all," he said, and groaned. "I tore my pants and butchered my leg."

"Eee-yoo," Val whined.

"It's only a scratch, for crissakes," Doug teased, holding out his hand. "Grab hold."

Charlie stood with Doug's assistance. "I'm butchered," he lamented. "I'll probably bleed to death…and look at my new jeans. Geez!"

Sam rolled her eyes and said, "C'mon, don't cry, it'll be okay."

"Hey, society boy," Val teased. "Don't you know better than to wear new clothes out here in the boonies?"

Everyone looked at Charlie and then burst out laughing.

"Okay," Charlie said with a weak grin, "I guess I deserved that."

"Is that what you tripped over?" Sam asked, pointing to something big and bulky surrounded by weeds.

They walked over to look. “Oh, crap!” Val cupped her mouth and quick-stepped back.

“Duuurn,” Doug drawled. “That’s it! That’s the chopping block!” He tapped the map. “See, it shows the stump lined up with the corner of the wall. This has got to be it!”

“Durned if it ain’t,” Charlie said in a low, wondrous voice. “Look, the ax marks are still visible.”

The huge lighter pine stump stood about two feet high and three feet wide and was surrounded by tall weeds. Well-defined marks, like those left by an ax, were clearly noticeable.

Doug squatted down to get a closer look. “See this?” With his finger he traced an outline of something dark.

“Blood stains!”

“Oh!” Val’s fingers flew to her mouth. “Do you think it really is … blood?”

“Sure, blood will soak into wood and turn it dark,” Doug explained. “See how it widened out, then ran over the edge? And look here.” He pointed to splotches of darkness on the stump. “That must have been where the blood splattered.”

The mood turned somber, even for Doug. They stood gawking at the execution spot.

“Look at the sun,” Charlie pointed out. “We’re gonna get caught in here after dark if we don’t hurry.”

The purpling western sky allowed shadows to slowly merge with approaching darkness. The treetops caught the radiance of the sun, creating a surreal skyline.

Something moved.

Sam’s head snapped around. “What was that? I saw something move—over there.” She pointed to a stand of pine near the riverbank. “It sorta zipped from one tree to another.”

“Probably an animal…a deer maybe,” Doug said.

“No,” she replied, “I saw something…and it looked like a man. …I know I did.”

Val said, “Maybe it was a tiger.”

Everyone turned and stared. In the fading light her blonde

hair was suddenly conspicuous.

"What!" Sam sniped, giving her a "don't be stupid" look. "Like, this is North America?"

"Whatever," was Val's quick reply.

"Come on," Doug said, motioning them along, "let's go find the steps."

He led off and the others reluctantly followed like baby ducks.

Wagon ruts marked where Main Street once ran. Remnants of a sidewalk lay in decaying pieces. Magnolia and rosebud trees, decorated in innocent white and scarlet red, still lined the dead street.

"There it is!" Charlie exclaimed, seeing them first.

The teens walked reverently, as if the steps were somehow sacred. Black mildew and green algae covered the pitted cement.

"Just think," Charlie whispered, "people once walked on these very steps."

A church steeple, partly hidden by weeds, lay on its side, its spire digging into the earth.

"Look, that's it!" Doug said, excited. "The graveyard … come on, let's check it out."

"I'm not going in there," Sam said, shaking her head.

"Me either," Val confirmed.

Charlie snapped his fingers. "So much for making out in the graveyard." He seemed genuinely disappointed.

"Come on, Charlie, let's go see if we can find Hattie's grave," Doug said, turning to leave. "The scaredy-cats can stay here where it's safe."

"What?" Sam said. "No way are you leaving us here by ourselves." She caught Doug's arm and scooted up next to him.

Val thrust her arm around Charlie's.

Sunken and leaning tombstones looked ghoulish in the shadowed light. Doug felt pleased. This was the effect he had wanted, vampire-ish and scary. He couldn't have asked for anything better.

"The map shows Hattie's grave in the back corner, away

from the main cemetery," Doug said, pointing to the well-defined X on the Yahoo map.

Doug, Sam, Charlie and Val worked their way around the weathered tombstones and crypts. No one had been interred there for at least a hundred years, the last burial having occurred in 1908.

"The map shows the grave over there," Doug said, pointing to the northwest corner of the graveyard.

They trudged through the wiry grass toward Hattie's resting place.

"It's so foggy," Sam noted.

The explorers looked around. To their surprise, fog had rolled in from the river and quickly covered Traders Hill with a horror-movie haze.

Doug, even more pleased, wrung his hands and grinned. *Perfect*, he thought. Doug had always been fascinated with the macabre. Horror movies were his favorite genre. He'd seen them all, *Dracula*, *Frankenstein*, *Halloween,* and what he considered the best horror movie ever made, *Nightmare on Elm Street*.

Valerie stumbled, emitting an "Ooofff," and fell. "Oh, my head!" she said, groaning.

"Valerie!" Charlie dropped to his knees and slipped his hands around her waist. He helped her into a sitting position. "My God, you're hurt!"

Blood trickling from a cut on her forehead was already running down her cheek.

Reaching down to help, Sam asked, "Are you all right, Val?"

"Look! You've found it," Doug nearly yelled. "Hattie's grave. See?"

A faded tombstone leaned sideways in the sunken dirt.

Valerie, still in the sitting position, stared directly at the writing:

Hattie Jenkins
1867 – 1898
Murderer

Nearby bushes moved.

"Oh my God, what was that?" Val said, grabbing hold of Charlie's arm.

Another movement.

Sam screamed.

A muffled laugh.

Charlie yanked Val to her feet. "Let's get out of here!"

"Now!" Doug grabbed Sam by the hand.

Val wobbled.

"Hold on to me," Charlie cried.

She leaned into him for support.

The fog had gotten thicker.

A screeching laugh.

The teenagers stumbled through wire grass and weaved around tombstones.

The cackling got louder.

"I have to rest," Val cried out.

"We can't stop now," said Charlie, holding her tighter.

"Look," Doug shouted, "the steps—we're getting closer to the street."

Behind them … footsteps!

Doug and Sam zipped into the street and headed for the landing … and the boat.

Charlie and Val stumbled close behind.

"I can't go on," Val whimpered as they reached the steps. "I have to …" Val's legs gave way and she collapsed.

Charlie, too tired to hold her up, collapsed alongside her and yelled, "Doug … help me!"

Doug and Sam staggered to a stop. "They're in trouble," he said. "We have to go back."

Heinous laughter echoed from the graveyard.

"Down here," Charlie cried. "In front of the steps."

Doug and Sam, out of breath, crumpled beside their friends.

Footsteps approached.

"Who's there," Doug demanded.

Laughter.

The two boys peeked from behind the crumbling steps.

Something terrible was walking toward them.

"Ooooh," Doug groaned.

Hattie held her ax high. A wrinkled hand with long bony fingers clutched her head in its palm. She moved closer.

The terrified youths mewled with fear.

Dead milky eyes stared from a craggy face with protruding tongue. Long stringy hair, matted and filthy, fell over her arm. She pulled the ax over her shoulder. The dull blade pointed skyward.

"Noooo!" Doug screamed while snatching Sam to one side as the ax fell. "Run!"

They couldn't. Val sat scrunched against a step, too weak to move.

The ax swung.

Charlie grabbed Val by her arm and pulled.

Thwack!

Just in time, Val had staggered to her feet and Charlie lifted her in his arms and ran, with Doug and Sam beside them.

Through the fog the landing came into view. A sign lying near the docks read "Welcome to Traders Hill" in faded black letters.

The teens reached the river. Val's breath was labored. Her head, blue and swollen, still bled.

They prepared to leap over the bulkhead to the waiting boat.

The river lapped against the pilings.

"It's gone," Doug cried. "The boat's gone!"

The incoming tide had taken it away.

Heinous laughter erupted behind them.

Again, Hattie lifted her ax.

* * *

The four teens, wet and tired, drifted downriver with the

tide.

Their only choice had been to jump into the water. Charlie, a strong swimmer, had held on to Val.

Luck had been on their side. The boat, after floating free, had moved downriver a short distance and then become entangled in marsh grass.

Though exhausted, they had managed to clamber onboard. Doug hit the starter and the Evinrude roared to life.

"Just look at my shoes, Charlie," Val said with a weak smile. "Tomorrow you're taking me to the mall."

"The Pappy Camp" is a story about a man who lived in Lafayette County, Florida, until his death in the '60s. He was a relative of the author's lifelong friend, Keith Dampier, one of the characters in the Five Points Spook Club stories in this book. This story was related by his Grandfather Bennett.

Taft Calhoun lived in a shack without electricity or plumbing during the Great Depression. He did "wrassle" alligators for their hides and the Pappy Camp was a real place. Taft always stood by his story as the truth.

"Crybaby Bridge" is an urban myth that originally came out of South Carolina. Ohio, Texas and Maryland also claim to have their own Crybaby Bridge. The author adapted it to a bridge over the Suwannee River in Deep Creek, Florida, a community in Columbia County a few miles north of his old Five Points neighborhood.

Dedicated as the Fred P. Cone Bridge after Florida's twenty-seventh governor, also of Columbia County, it was also known as the Burn-Out Bridge and had a long and colorful history. A section of the old wooden structure gave way to a log truck, plunging it into the Suwannee and killing its driver. Finally after years of neglect, a fire ravaged what was left of the rotting timbers.

THE PAPPY CAMP

"I'll tell you the story about the puppies, but you probably won't believe me."

"Try me, Mr. Taft."

The *Mayo Free Press*, a small-town newspaper in Mayo, Florida, published regular articles in their Lifestyle section, spotlighting local citizens. Taft Calhoun, a lifelong resident, was to be the featured "person of interest" for an upcoming edition.

"It's quite a tale, from what I hear," said Ira Taylor, from the *Press*. "You have an excellent reputation in Lafayette County, Mr. Calhoun. Nobody, including me, has any reason to doubt you."

Taft smiled and leaned forward in his rocking chair. "Ghost puppies—yes sir, spotty ghost puppies at that—that's what they were."

"You saw spotty ghost puppies?"

"Yessir, but those ghost puppies were nothing compared to what I saw next."

"You've got my attention," Ira said, using crossed legs as a desk for his steno pad.

"Like to have scared me to death, not to mention my old mare, Ruby," Taft said, giving his rocking chair a nudge. "That thing stood right beside me. Right on the wagon seat."

Ira stopped writing.

"Yessir." Taft leaned forward. "I've never been so scared in my life. Not before, nary since."

* * *

"Back during the Great Depression, things was rough, jobs scarce. Hard to make a living in those days. … Yessir, mighty hard to make a living."

Ira continued taking notes, shaking his head in agreement.

"I grew what crops I could, foraged for wild onion and polk salad in the fields and swamps, kept a few chickens and an old milk cow. But we made it with nary a complaint or help from the guv'ment."

"How did you earn money for staples, shoes, things like that?" asked Ira.

"Gator hides … sold gator hides. Used to knock 'im in the head with a club so I wouldn't flaw 'em. Brought a better price that way."

"Fascinating!"

"Used to wrassle 'em, right in the water."

"You really did that?"

"As I'm living and breathing."

"When I was a kid, I heard stories about you all the time. Why, you were a real hero to us kids."

Taft smiled. "After I collected a couple of gators, I'd skin 'em, then stretch their hides out to dry. Ate the tail, too. Didn't throw nothing away."

"Was it good?" Ira asked, making a frown.

"It *didn't* taste like chicken, if that's what you're asking. But it was passable, better than no meat at all."

"Tell me about the Pappy Camp."

"In those days, a lot of people made a living dippin' turpentine …"

"Dipping?"

"That was the word they used," Taft explained. "The men would scrape the bark from a pine tree, score the wood with a hatchet, then stick a wedge in, usually a piece of tin, so the sap would drain onto it. Then they hung a bucket underneath the tin to catch the sap."

"What would they do with the sap once the buckets were full?" Ira asked, enthralled with the old man.

"The sap was poured into barrels, then taken to a distillery for processing."

Ira continued to write on his steno.

"Of course, the men lived in camps where they slept in bedrolls or under lean-to tents on a bed of pine straw. For entertainment they would tell stories around a campfire until bedtime. A little shut-eye and it was back to the woods for another day's work."

Ira interrupted, saying, "And one of those camps was the Pappy Camp?"

"Named after Pappy Goodbread, the man who owned the property. You gittin' all this down, young man?"

"Yes sir, I sure am."

"Well, one day I went to the swamp real early to get a jump on the heat. When I passed the camp, I noticed all the men had already taken to the woods. I usually stopped and had a cup of coffee, you know. So I went on down the road toward the swamp. Actually it weren't a road a-tall, only two wagon ruts." Taft paused a few moments to collect his thoughts.

"I went on down to the swamp and commenced my hunt for gators, eventually getting two old bulls. Had to wrassle 'em down. I was a big man back then, you know."

"How big were they?" Ira asked, totally enthralled.

"Oh, eight, nine feet maybe. Little things—felt ashamed of myself."

"You should have been!" said Ira.

Taft stopped in mid-rock, saw Ira's grin, slapped his leg and hooted. "Good one," he said.

"Just curious," Ira said. "What's it like in the swamp?"

"Hot, snake infested, mosquitoes eat you alive, dangerous—all that and more. But mostly, it's beautiful. Cypress trees covered with blue-gray moss, a thousand different plants, wildlife ranging from frogs to panthers, all living together creating a special world, unique and wonderful."

Ira was taken aback by Taft's eloquence. "You make it sound so grand."

"It is, and I miss it. … But I've never missed those puppies. … Well, to shorten the story. I threw the hides into my wagon and then Ruby and me headed home. I always talked to Ruby, but she was stubborn, never talked back, but was a very good listener. … Like I was saying, we were on the way home when Ruby got fidgety, her ears went to twitching, her head turned from one side to the other. She got this wild look in her eyes and before I knew it she was running like a scared rabbit.

"Whoa, I hollered. The wagon began to bounce, 'bout threw me out. I pulled on the reins so hard Ruby's head pointed toward the sky. Well, I finally got her stopped. Figgered she had been spooked by a snake. By the time I got her to calm down, we were a little ways past the Pappy Camp. I turned and looked to see if anybody had made it back from the woods. … That's when I saw them! Six white hounds with black and brown spots, barking, growling little puppy growls and jumping all over one another the way puppies do. They were the prettiest hounds I ever saw.

"Ruby was still fidgety, stomping her feet, pawing, whinnying. Couldn't figger it out. Anyhow, I set the wagon's brake and jumped down. I had to see those little hounds, hoping that just maybe, I could get one for myself. A good hunting dog was a cause for pride in those days.

"Well, I walked back the few yards to the camp. Dippin' buckets were scattered here and there, the scent of turpentine strong, the makeshift cook shack had firewood piled against it, everything was normal … except for that litter of spotty hounds."

Ira asked quickly, "Didn't it seem strange for a litter of puppies to be running loose?"

"What seemed strange was the camp. Everything was normal, like I said, except the feeling. It was spooky, spine-chill spooky.

"I walked right up to those puppies and squatted down. They paid me no mind at all, like I wasn't there. So I whistled and called, 'Here puppy, puppy, puppy.' Not a single one turned to look. Normally, puppies will wag their tails and sashay right on up to you. But not them.

"I reached over to pick one up. Whoosh! It vanished."

Ira exclaimed, "Vanished! You mean, like disappear?" He had stopped taking notes long ago.

"Exactly! But I shrugged it off as just being tired. Took me a while to wear them gators down, you know. So I reached again, this time with both hands. That little dog sorta faded right through my hands. That's when I got scared! Those puppies kept disappearing and then reappearing in different places.

"Ghost puppies!" I remember saying out loud. Hair on my arms stood straight out, my scalp prickled. Then I hollered like a sissy and hit the ground with my butt. Desperate to get away, I pushed with my heels and walked backward on my hands.

"Old Ruby was having a fit, rearing and trying to pull the wagon with the brake on. I jumped up but stumbled over a bucket and fell flat on my face. I rose to my knees and spit dirt out of my mouth. Then, I got the strangest feeling ... like I was being watched. I jerked around! All six hounds were staring at me. Their hackles stood up. They started growling through bared teeth! I ran, like a youngin' in the dark!"

Ira dropped his pad.

"I jumped up on the wagon, releasing the brake as I hit the seat. Ruby took off like a race horse. The wagon jerked and I tumbled backward, landing on the hides. Ruby was running flat-out, the wagon bouncing in and out of the ruts.

"Finally, after a lot of effort, I managed to climb back onto the seat. Then, fear—a trembling fear—went through my body like ice water!"

Ira's pencil clattered across the porch.

"I heard a low, throaty growl. I jerked around. … The old she-hound stood on the seat! Her eyes were raging wild. She bares her teeth … growls … lunges …"

"No!" Ira exclaimed, throwing his hands up.

"The wagon bounces into a tree. I sail through the air, land on my back, narrowly missing a pine stump."

Taft, letting out a deep breath, leaned back into his rocking chair.

Ira waited, but soon mumbled, "What happened?"

"I ran faster than I'd ever run in my life."

"What about Ruby?"

"She made it home five minutes after I did. Plum embarrassed her. Never looked me in the eyes again."

A smile slipped across Taft's craggy face.

CRYBABY BRIDGE

"Ever hear the story about Crybaby Bridge?" Rob asked his friend, Paul.

"Sure, that's the same bridge where the baby sat and cried because he spilled his milk. So the child's mother said, 'There, there, now. Don't cry over spilt milk.' "

"That's what I like about you," Rob said, "a crazy sense of humor."

"And the reason I'm crazy? Answer … because I hang out with you. So, tell me about the Spilt Milk Bridge."

"You're totally crazy—and it's Crybaby Bridge."

"Okay, so, go ahead, *spill* it."

Rob pushed the ORDER button on the Sonic Drive-In's intercom.

The tinny voice asked, "May I take your order?"

"One psychologist, clinical, white coat—hold the mayo."

"Uh, would you repeat that?"

"Two cheeseburgers, two fries and two Cokes."

"Okay, in the interest of proverbs, and your sanity, tell me about the bridge."

"Too late about the sanity part, but here goes." Rob draped his arm over the steering wheel. "Ever hear about the old wooden bridge over the Suwannee in the Deep Creek community?"

"Can't say that I have."

"It's supposedly haunted by a baby and its mother." Rob waited for a wisecrack.

"So, I'm listening."

"Oh, okay. James Prince married Clara Ann Bordeaux.

Together they built a house not far from Cone Bridge …"

"Cone Bridge?" Paul asked.

"Yeah, that's the bridge's official name, the Fred P. Cone Bridge. Cone was a hometown boy who made it all the way to the governor's office."

"Whoopty-doo."

"James and Clara had a little girl they named Mary Charlotte. Like, he had his own pulp wood truck, she kept house, took care of the baby. No problems, life was good, right?"

"If you say so," Paul quipped.

"Well, one night Clara and James went to bed, everything was normal …"

"Like us."

"No! Like *me*. Geez! As I said, they went to bed. Mary Charlotte was sleeping in her crib in the next room."

When they woke up the next morning Mary was gone. An early morning fisherman found her body underneath the bridge. Her gown had snagged on a piling, preventing her from floating downriver. She was only two months old."

"That's sad."

"The bedroom window was open and the screen off. Man-sized footprints were found outside the window. They figured she'd been kidnapped and thrown over the bridge."

"So, they found the person who did it—right?"

"Wrong," said Rob. "They never did. Clara, the baby's mother, was so distraught that she threw herself off the bridge and drowned."

"Does it get any sadder?"

"No, but it gets scary."

* * *

Rob and Paul trashed their cheeseburger wrappers and empty Coke cups and then rolled out of Sonic's parking lot. Rob's Ford pickup, radio belting out a Nirvana song, pointed north toward the Suwannee River.

"Hey, dude, you gonna finish the story?" asked Paul.

Rob punched off the radio. "The story goes like this: You park on the bridge, turn off the ignition, take the key out, roll down the window and wait for the baby to cry."

"Cool."

"And one more thing."

"I'm listening."

"Clara never knew who killed her baby, so she takes revenge on anyone who places their billfold on the hood and chants, 'I killed your baby' three times. The billfold will then fall off the hood, onto the bridge. Then her spirit rises out of the water, snatches the person who taunted her off the bridge and drags him into the river to drown. … Oh, and it has to be midnight."

"Naturally. Nine o'clock never works."

"The only way you can stop Clara's spirit from carrying out her revenge is to quickly say, 'I didn't kill your baby' three times. By doing that she will know that you're telling the truth."

"Better put down the hammer," Paul said. "It's eleven thirty, only thirty minutes till midnight."

A pastel moon spread light over the countryside. At the Five Points junction, five mud-covered Honda Recons crossed over to Gum Swamp Road, speeding toward Mild Branch.

"I wonder where those nuts are headed," Paul said.

With ten minutes to spare the Ford turned onto the narrow dirt road leading to the river. The twin I-beams, bouncing over the ungraded road, caused the pickup to shudder.

"Slow down, bro, before you put us in the ditch," Paul cautioned.

Off the road not far from the river stood an old house under the shade of a mossy live oak, its roof caved in and its walls sagging in decay. The Ford and its teenaged passengers rattled past Clara and James Prince's former home.

"There it is," Rob said. "Crybaby Bridge."

Rusty steel trusses spanned the wooden bridge that sat high on the bluff, looking ghostly and forlorn in the moonlight. Below, streaks of light and shadow covered the river.

"Spooky," Paul admitted.

Slowly, Rob drove onto the bridge. The old timbers creaked and groaned under the truck's weight. Reaching the middle, Rob switched off the headlights and killed the engine. Both boys rolled down their windows.

They waited. The sounds of frogs and crickets invaded the still night. An owl hooted.

Then Rob noticed. "Here's the problem. Forgot to take the key out of the ignition." Slipping the key out, he placed it on the console.

Immediately they heard it.

Soft whimpering, like a baby waking from a nap, broke the stillness.

Rob whispered, "Hear that?"

"I don't believe it … it can't be."

"Shush." Rob put an index finger over his mouth. "Listen."

Whimpering turned to sobs. The familiar cries of a baby floated through the air.

"Come on," Rob whispered, opening the door and stepping out onto the bridge.

The boards squeaked.

Paul followed.

Both doors remained open, the dome light casting jagged shadows around the truck.

Rob signaled for Paul to meet him at the rail.

The cries continued, sounding distant and weak.

Paul crossed in front of the truck, joining Rob at the bridge's rail. Steel support cables angled down from corroding trusses, attaching to thick timbers on the bridge proper.

Rob whispered, "I can't tell where it's coming from."

FORD

"Me either."

The baffled teens bent over the guardrails and cupped their ears.

"I can hear it a little better," Paul said in a hoarse voice, "but I can't tell exactly where it's coming from."

The cries were intermittent, restless and haunting.

Then the teens pinpointed the sounds.

Paul murmured, "Underneath the bridge."

"The piling!"

Barely audible, Rob said, "The time!" He pushed a button on his digital watch and a light flashed on. The numbers flicked over to twelve.

"You gonna say it?" Paul asked.

"Nuh … uh, not me, bro."

"Well, okay, I'll say it." Paul started to repeat the chant when he remembered, "Better put my wallet on the hood." He eased his wallet from his Wranglers and placed it on the Ford. He cupped his hand to his mouth. "I killed your baby—I killed your baby—I killed your baby!"

They waited. Nothing happened.

Paul started to repeat the chant and the wallet slid from the hood.

Paul and Rob spun around.

A voice called out, "Who killed my baby?"

The boys gasped.

The ghost of Clara Ann Prince rose slowly above the bridge. Her long white gown shimmered in the pale light. She stood still in midair, just above the guardrail. Her arms stretched. Her glaring eyes focused on Paul.

"You killed my baby!"

"I didn't kill—"

Clara snatched Paul, pulling him over the railing and plunging him into the river.

The crying stopped.

Rob yelled, backed up and fell, sprawling on his back.

The dome light illuminated his horror-stricken face.

Pushing up, he crabbed backward, his hands filling with splinters. His back pushed flush against the front wheel. Spinning around, Rob leapt to his feet and dove through the open door.

"The key!"

A thought struck him. Grabbing the key from the console, Rob shoved it into the ignition. The eight-cylinder engine jumped to life.

Shoving it into reverse he stomped the gas. The truck lunged backward.

The passenger door remained open. The pickup swerved, slamming the open door into the railing. The door bent, smashing it into the front fender.

The Ford flew off the bridge, bouncing as it met the road. Rob lost control and the truck veered and hit a tree. Rob shot forward, slamming his head against the steering wheel.

Dazed but not seriously hurt, he rammed the automatic into DRIVE and shoved the accelerator to the floor. Dirt splattered against tree bark, the truck fishtailed … then tires gripped the road, sending the Ford away from the bridge.

* * *

Guilty tears flowed as Rob drove down the highway. Suddenly, with a flash of defiance he whipped the truck around in the middle of the highway. The smashed door flopped and banged against the cab.

Swinging onto the dirt road, he thrust the pedal to the floor. The Ford snaked from side to side, barely missing the ditches. Finally, to keep from losing control, he forced himself to slow down.

The bobbing headlights caught the reflection of something in the road.

Rob couldn't believe it. Paul stood soaking wet in the middle of the road, waving his arms.

Rob applied the brakes, squeaking the battered truck to a halt.

"Need a ride?" Rob asked.

Paul said, "Not unless you're going the other way."

A HAUNTING TALE

"Wallpaper," a dream the author had one restless night, resulted in this haunting tale set in a Civil War–era mansion. Of course dreams don't come true.

Or do they?

WALLPAPER

The voices pleaded from behind the heavy oak door. Adam held the key, but his hand trembled as he aimed it at the keyhole.

Voices from behind the door wailed—like a room full of cheering people sounding eager, even happy.

Adam hesitated … then backed away. The voices fell, moaning disappointment.

Sweat broke out on his forehead.

He shoved in the key.

The voices rose to a crescendo.

Adam jerked his hand away.

The voices died, followed by silence. Like someone holding their breath … waiting … anticipating ….

He flung the door open.

Adam woke with a jerk, gasping for breath.

* * *

"Are you out of your mind?" Chris said. "I ain't about to go anywhere near that crypt. Gives me the creepies just to think about it."

"Look," Adam said, "you know I wouldn't ask if it wasn't important."

"What's so important about going to a spooky old house?"

"I told you about the dreams, right?"

"Yeah …"

"And how, in those dreams I can't quite get the courage to unlock the door to the mysterious room?"

"Yeah, so. …"

"So, the dreams keep coming back. I feel like I'll keep having them until I actually go to the house and open that door."

"Didn't your parents tell you not to *ever* go there?"

"Yeah, so?"

"So, you should mind your parents."

"Hey, I'm a teenager. I'm expected to disobey my parents. I owe it to the teens of the world. Seriously, they're going to Atlanta this weekend. They'll never know."

Chris said, "How long has it been since anybody lived there, anyway?"

"I don't know, maybe seventy-five years? It's been in the family since before the Civil War. My dad's great-grandfather, Isaiah Hardee, was the last person to live there. He left a will strictly forbidding anyone to ever live there again."

"Couldn't your dad sell it?"

"The will stated it was to never be sold. He left a trust fund just to keep the taxes paid."

"Have you ever been inside?"

Adam shook his head. "No, never have. When I was about ten, my grandfather died and left the mansion to Dad. He had never been allowed to go there while Poppa was living, but was never told why. One day he decided to check it, and took me with him.

"Once we got there, he unlocked the gate and we drove on up to the house. Immediately I felt the impulse to go inside. Dad sat in the car for the longest time, just staring—like he was trying to make up his mind whether he should go in or not. Then he started to shake. His eyes got big as saucers, like he'd seen a ghost, or something worse. I have never seen Dad scared before, but he was really scared that day. We left and neither of us has ever been back, except for the time you and I rode out there and peeked through the fence."

Chris shuddered. "Yeah, and it really creeped me out—and we were outside the gate!"

"So, you coming?"

"Yeah, no problem. I can only be scared to death once, right?"

"Yes!" Adam high-fived his friend. "I knew I could count on you, bro. You can crash at my place tonight so we can get an early start in the morning."

* * *

Adam and Chris rode in the blue and gray Dodge Hemi with the windows open, taking in the coolness of the morning. They rode through the countryside, down a two-lane paved road, the sweet scent of jasmine swirling through the cab. A rusty barbed-wire fence supported a bank of morning glory vines in full bloom and farm crops grew in straight rows with the promise of tasty meals to come.

It was only a ten-minute drive from Adam's house to the abandoned Hardee estate. The next thing they knew the truck was heading down the road that led back to the southern mansion.

"You do have the key to those padlocks, right?" Chris asked.

"And the key to the house," Adam said, jangling a ring of keys. "What I don't have, though, is the key to the upstairs room; it's in the mansion somewhere. We have to find it."

"Nervous?" asked Chris.

"A little."

"Me too, but at least we're going during the day instead of at the stroke of midnight."

Chris could tell that Adam was more than a little nervous by the way he gripped the steering wheel. His knuckles were white from lack of circulation.

Rounding the last curve, Adam announced, "Well, there it is."

Chris leaned forward like a dog scrutinizing a stranger, "Looks like a crypt."

Heavy chains clattered against the wrought-iron gate as Chris pulled the padlocks free. The Dodge passed through and Chris climbed back into the passenger seat. Adam drove so slowly, the truck looked like a cat sneaking up on its prey.

"We can always go back, you know," Chris said. "You don't have to go in there."

"That's just it. I do. If I don't, those crazy dreams aren't going away."

"You mean nightmares."

"Exactly!"

The truck squeaked to a stop. They pushed the doors open, making the truck resemble a blue bird in flight. They waited. Then, reluctantly, the teens slipped off the truck seats, shutting the doors behind them.

Adam held on to the black door handle while staring at the old house. Roof shingles were missing. The windows, cloudy with years of grime, were covered with heavy drapes inside. Slivers of white paint still hung to life on the bare wood.

"Ready?" Adam asked.

"No!"

"That makes two of us."

Adam took a few steps toward the house and Chris followed close behind.

A sound, like distant waves lapping the seashore, seeped from the upstairs window.

"What's that noise?" Chris asked.

Adam's eyes instantly focused on the upstairs window. "That's it! The sounds I hear in my dreams, only ..."

A macabre feeling swept over them.

"Oh!" Adam jerked to a stop.

"Oooh!" Chris whimpered. "Did you feel that?"

"Yeah, I felt it, something changed, like we're being warned away or something."

"Maybe we are, maybe there's a reason your great-grandfather didn't want anybody near this place. Ever think of that?"

"I know he had his reasons, but what? And what does it have to do with those crazy dreams? I feel like something is drawing me here and at the same time that something is trying to keep me away … and the secret is behind that locked door. I have to find out."

"Adam, be real, bro, this could be something way over your head."

"Maybe, but I have to do this. You can wait here. … No problem, okay? I understand."

Chris stared at the draped upstairs window where the muffled sounds came from. "Nuh-uh, no way are you getting rid of me that easily."

Adam's shoulders sagged with relief, happy that his best friend was with him.

They started toward the house again. The yard was overgrown with briers and weeds. Statues of cherubs stood guard over a young girl playing the violin and a boy playing flute. The cement figures were pitted and discolored from years of wind, rain and relentless sun.

The morbid feeling persisted.

"Look at that!" Adam whined, scrutinizing the house. "It looks like something dead. I don't remember it looking this run-down."

"Don't say d-e-a-d."

Together they climbed the steps. Two lions sat on pedestals guarding the entrance. The neoclassical mansion's wide porch was supported by four Ionic columns resting on a rounded base and reaching to the second-floor balcony. The tops were decorated with scroll-shaped ornaments resembling a ram's horn.

The boys shuffled to the door.

"Ah!" Adam bent over, holding his stomach. The keys jangled to the porch floor.

Chris pushed back against a column and groaned, his mouth gaped open.

A force, dark and sinister, gripped them like a shroud.

They weakened instantly.

The droning voices grew louder and louder, until it sounded like a stadium full of indistinguishable voices cheering their team on.

Recovering from the sudden attack Adam slowly straightened up and moaned, “You okay, Chris?”

“Okay, I guess,” he said in a whispery voice. His skin had turned sallow.

A discolored brass knocker with a lion’s head still clung to the heavy oak door. Decorative swirly designs were carved above the doorway, with the Roman numerals MDCCCL.

Chris pointed at it and said, “So 1850 is when this old crypt was built.”

“I don’t think it was built, it just came into existence, like something evil.”

Adam picked up the key ring and fumbled for the door key. He chose a long, slender one with an eye on the finger-grip end and two square teeth at the other. He slipped it in. Click! The tumblers disengaged. He grasped the doorknob and turned. Cling! The bolt sprang from the door jamb.

Adam glanced at Chris. He nodded his head and Adam gave the heavy door a shove. It labored, creaking halfway open.

The teens tiptoed through the doorway as if to sneak past anything that might be lurking within.

The crowd had stopped cheering; the house was silent.

Holding his nostrils closed, Chris said, “Eee-you, it stinks in here.”

Stale, musty air from mold, rot and years of accumulated dust overpowered their lungs, causing them to cough. Their eyes watered.

Slam!

Adam jerked around.

“Sorry,” Chris said with a sheepish grin. “Pushed the door a little too hard.”

"Geez! Thanks a lot! I think I wet my pants."

"It's dark in here," Chris said. "Come on, let's pull open the drapes and let some light in."

"Open that door again, too. You know, just in case."

Adam and Chris pulled the drape cords. The rollers squeaked and tugged the royal blue cloth into bunches, causing dust to swirl about the room. Eventually, sunlight swathed the cavernous hall.

The furniture stood uncovered, left the way it was the day Isaiah Hardee had died. On the far wall a fireplace with half-burnt logs lay amidst piles of ashes. Above the mantel a painting of Lt. Gen. Amos Hardee posed proudly in his Confederate uniform, one of the young men in Jefferson Davis's rebel army.

"What now?" asked Chris.

"Let's go upstairs."

* * *

Curving mahogany banisters lined the wide staircase leading to the second floor. The boys climbed, stepping lightly to test the strength of the wood. Each step creaked and groaned like an arthritic old man with bad knees.

They stepped into the second-floor hallway. All doors were open, exposing bed, bath and sitting rooms—all, that is, but one. Their gaze immediately shifted to a dark oak door at the far end of the vestibule.

"There it is! Oh!" Adam gasped. Seeing the door of his nightmares sent chills throughout his body. His legs wobbled as he walked, with trepidation, wondering what secrets lay there.

Chris followed one step behind, murmuring under his breath.

Then they stood facing the door.

An overwhelming power seized them. Thick darkness shrouded their minds. They couldn't speak. Their knees buckled, sending them prostrate on the floor.

From behind the great door, voices rose in a chant: "Adam, Adam, Adam, Adam!"

Whatever had power over the boys relaxed its grip. The voices droned on. Then with renewed force the sinister power fought back until they were completely wrapped in darkness.

"Adam, Adam, Adam!" The chants became increasing louder: "Adam, Adam, Adam!"

The mysterious power and chanting voices fought for control.

The voices won.

The shroud of darkness lifted like a veil. Adam and Chris slowly regained their strength and pulled themselves from the hardwood floor. Their legs wobbled and they held on to each other for support.

"Wh-what happened?" Chris asked, his voice strained.

"Something's trying to keep me—uh, us—from whatever's in that room."

"The voices," Chris noted. "I don't hear them anymore."

Adam reached for the doorknob.

"The key, the key, the key!" came the voices.

"Key … where?"

"The desk, the desk, the desk!" the voices answered.

At the other end of the hall an open door revealed an antique rolltop desk.

"There," Adam cried.

The boys moved slowly down the hall, still weak from their bizarre encounter with the mysterious force.

They entered the musty room. Sunlight from open drapes revealed a spacious study, its walls lined with bookshelves. A round table held pictures of long-dead relatives and a grandfather clock stood catty-cornered, the time, three fifteen, frozen on its face. The desk sat near a small window. Chris pulled open the curtain.

Adam said, "The key must be in here." He grabbed the handle on the rolltop and pushed.

Dust flew as slatted wood folded into the desk's top. Pigeonholes were crammed with old receipts and bills. A ledger was spread open. A long, slender key lay on the right-hand page. Under the key, a handwritten note:

> *If you've found this key, it means you are a Hardee, and you alone have been chosen because of your courage and because it is time. The Hardee family has waited so long for this nightmare curse to end. You will know what to do.*
>
> *Isaiah Hardee*

"So, I *was* led here," Adam said. "Those dreams *did* mean something!"

Chris looked him in the eyes and said, "What do you intend to do?"

"I don't know, but I have a feeling the answer is behind that door."

* * *

Adam stood at the heavy oak door, key in hand. He had doubts. What if he opened the door and found something terrible there? What if that entity of darkness he had encountered a few minutes ago now waited on the other side of the door? What if . . .

But the voices pleaded from behind the locked door.

Adam's hand trembled. What if . . .

He snatched his hand away and started to turn around.

The wailing voices fell, moaning disappointment.

Just like in his dream. But he knew it had to be done.

The key slipped into the hole with a metallic rasp.

Click!

He flung open the door.

Silence.

A shaft of light crossed the floor, revealing a draped window.

"I'll open it," Chris volunteered, and stepped in.

Adam followed.

Then they saw it. A silent, shadowy mass hovered in the corner, spinning like a cyclone.

Adam whimpered, "Oh!"

It rushed across the room, completely engulfing him.

Darkness bound him like chains. His energy slipped away.

"Adam, Adam, Adam," the voices cried from one side of the room.

"Courage, courage, courage," they called from the other side.

The dark power struggled for control.

"Adam, Adam, Adam!"

"Courage, courage, courage!"

The words slipped through his mind-fog, and Adam fought back.

The chanting rose to a deafening roar.

The power faded and the darkness ebbed. Then, with a screech the twirling shadow fled.

Light flooded the room.

Then silence.

* * *

Chris stood at the window, hand on the draw cord. Adam steadied himself and tried to focus.

Hundreds of eyes stared.

Chris walked gingerly to where Adam stood, his eyes scanning each wall. Chris whispered, "What *is* this?"

Adam mumbled, "Wallpaper … living wallpaper."

The paneled walls simulated wallpaper. Faces were embedded in the paneling, surrounded by decorative flowers carved into the wood … funeral flowers … roses, baby's breath, and red, blue and yellow lilies.

The boys turned in circles, scanning each wall while stepping softly, mouths open … speechless.

The imprisoned eyes followed every step.

A voice shouted, "Adam!"

The boys jerked around.

"Look at me," the voice implored.

The boys stared at the image. The name etched into the wood read:

Isaiah Hardee

1853 – 1942

Isaiah's eyes glared at the far wall. "Over there," he said.

Adam followed his gaze. At the far corner was an empty space. With slow and deliberate steps Adam walked toward it.

A name was inscribed onto the wall:

Adam Lee Hardee

1991 –

Adam gasped.

Chris said, "B-bro, that's you!"

"Yes, Adam, that's you," the voice said. "That's where you will be entombed in misery and torment … unless you stop it. Look around this awful room. It's filled with the imprisoned spirits of Hardees, your ancestors."

Adam examined the paneled wallpaper. Names of dead relative were inscribed under each image, beginning with Amos Hardee, the Civil War soldier.

"I brought on the curse," the image said. "By the way I treated my slaves. Because of me, the Hardee dead have been enslaved and tormented for generations."

Adam saw a name he knew. "Aunt Peg?" he said.

"Yes, Adam, it's me," she said with tears in her eyes. "We … all of us here still have all of our feelings we had in life. That's what has made it so bad. Now, my dear nephew, it's up to you to free us."

"But how?"

"Fire," she said.

"Fire," the wallpaper dead repeated in unison. Then they chanted, "Fire, fire, fire!" The chanting rose in pitch. "Fire, fire, fire!"

"Now!" Amos said.

"The kitchen!" Aunt Peg directed.

Adam knew what he had to do.

"Come on, Chris, let's go!"

The boys bolted from the room and shot down the stairs.

"The kitchen," Adam said. "Got to find the kitchen!"

"Why?"

"A pot—bucket—anything!"

"Back there, I think."

The voices chanted encouragement.

Adam and Chris ran through the great room toward the back of the house.

Adam yelled, "Here it is!"

"And there's a bucket."

Once used for canning vegetables, it sat on the top shelf of the open pantry.

"Grab it," Adam ordered. "I'm going to the groundskeeper's shed."

Chris grabbed the bucket by its handle. Screeching as the wire handle pulled up, the sound reverberated loudly out of the hollow pail.

Adam located the gardening shack. "Chris," he yelled, "Come help."

The bottom of the door was barricaded by grass and dirt, caused by years of nonuse.

"Help me pull," Adam said.

Chris dropped the bucket and wedged his hands between the door and frame. Adam already had a narrow handhold.

Adam said, "Ready … go!"

They snatched. The redoubt of grass and dirt ripped apart as the door scraped along the ground, creating an opening wide enough for the boys to squeeze through.

Chris asked, "What are you looking for?"

"A hose … anything I can siphon with."

"There," Chris said. "Talk about luck!"

A section of black hose lay rolled up underneath a pile of junk covered with dust and spider webs. Chris threw off some of the junk and yanked it free.

"Bring it," Adam shouted, "I'll grab the bucket."

"Hurry, hurry, hurry! Courage, courage, courage!"

Adam and Chris raced to the front of the mansion where the truck was parked. Adam fumbled to get the gas cap off.

Chris shoved one end of the hose down the tank's throat. Adam grabbed the other end, stuck it in his mouth, dirt and all. He drew with quick, successive breaths, attempting to extract gas from the tank.

Unleaded regular filled his mouth. He gagged and spat, gasping for air, at the same time aiming the hose toward the bucket. It soon filled to the rim.

Chris yanked the hose from the tank, stopping the flow of gasoline.

"Matches, I need matches. Glovebox—quick!"

Chris scrounged around until he found a book. "Here!" he said, shoving it toward Adam.

"Stay here!"

"But—"

"I won't be long, just do it!"

Adam grabbed the bucket of gasoline. He leaned to one side while taking quick, short steps, trying to hold the bucket away from his body to avoid getting splashed.

The voices pleaded, "Hurry, hurry, hurry!"

Adam passed the lion sentinels and stepped onto the porch. Gasoline splashed on the concrete.

"Courage, courage, courage," the voices wailed, sounding like a crowd of cheering fans. "Defense, defense, defense!"

Adam scuttled to the staircase.

He froze, fear surging through him.

An angry mass of revolving shadow blocked his passage. Beady red eyes peered out of a shapeless head.

Not a sound seeped from the wallpapered tomb.

Adam glared at the shadowy demon. Immediately he was seized upon by some power.

"Courage!"

He resisted.

"Courage!"

The shadow's red eyes burned like a pit of fire.

"Courage!"

Thick darkness gathered around Adam. His knees weakened. The power tried to bind him.

"Courage!"

Adam fought back.

The shadow refused to release him.

"Courage!"

"No!" Adam shouted with renewed resolve and stepped into the light.

The shadow threw back its formless head and shrieked. Then it was gone.

* * *

Smiles crossed the faces of the entombed dead as Adam entered. All eyes turned toward the old soldier. They waited.

"Well done," Amos said. "Well done, indeed."

Adam nodded and then tipped the bucket, spilling gasoline onto the floor. It snaked its way across the room to the far wall. An approving roar rushed from the wallpaper.

"Courage," he said, stepping from the crypt.

He made his way down the stairs, splashing fuel as he went.

Adam dropped the empty bucket and lit a match. He tossed it to the floor.

In a whoosh the fire roared up the staircase.

Adam ran out of the burning mansion toward the truck.

Chris pointed and said, "Look!"

Adam turned around. Spirits of his kindred dead rose like

wavy beams of light from the fire and then passed out of sight over the treetops … free at last.

Adam looked over at Chris and gave him a playful jab. “I’m bushed,” he said. “You drive.”

Chris fired off the Hemi and pointed it toward the highway. “I’m hungry,” he said, “how ’bout some hot wings?”

Adam glared at his friend. “*Hot* wings, you say? How about a hamburger instead?”

AUTHOR'S NOTE

"Jack-in-the-Box Clown" and "Ghost Soldiers" are stories told from my oldest daughter's perspective. Although in her thirties, she is adamant about seeing the jack-in-the-box float over her head and a soldier with a gun and bayonet standing in the corner of her room at her grandparents' home when she was a little girl. The story around those sightings, whether real or imagined, came from my imagination.

In "The Railroad Spikes," the spikes mysteriously appearing across the rails really did happen. I know … I was there. It happened several times as a group and while I was alone. I can't explain it but I'm sure there has to be a logical explanation. I don't want to know; it would take all the fun and mystery out of it. The part about the two boys in 1951 was my creation to build a story. The chrome plant is real, the people are real and Five Points is a real neighborhood.

"The Glowing House" existed. I have been there and have explored the empty rooms. The old house always seemed to be surrounded by a globe of light. Perhaps it was the way it sat with the forest as a backdrop.

My friends and I, on two occasions, saw a creature as described in "Demon Eyes." We were, on one occurrence, standing around talking late one night on the fringe of Andrew's Swamp. The creature ran across an adjacent field toward us. Not knowing what it was, the four of us jumped on the hood and roof of my '62 Chevy. The creature, or animal, ran around the car and scurried back across the field. Was it just a wild animal? Maybe, maybe not.

In "Ghost Wagon and Horse Bones" I told about the legend of the horse and wagon falling into the spring. Supposedly it happened. While swimming one evening, I, along with Keith, Joe Rea and Randy, saw—or thought we saw—the outline of a wagon on the bottom of the spring. Believe it or not, a piece of wood shot from the spring's bottom, drifted across the water and ended up in the Suwannee River where Branford Spring empties.

In "Weeping Woman Well," Alligator Lake is real and, upon occasion, the sinkhole opens and the lake drains. The history about the Indian village, Chief Tuskenuggee and Lake City are true. The Indian mounds are there and protected by the state of Florida.

Traders Hill was once a bustling town on the banks of the St. Marys River in Georgia, not far from the Okefenokee Swamp. The town disappeared with the advent of the railroad, the death knell of river trade. The cemetery is still there. My stepson, Michael Todd, related the story about the "witch" in "The Witch of Traders Hill." "The Secret of Traders Hill" came solely from my imagination.

"The Pappy Camp" is a story related to Keith by his Grandfather Bennett. Taft Calhoun, who died in the early '60s, stuck to his story about the ghost puppies until the end.

Many towns in America have a "Crybaby Bridge" legend told in many forms. I first heard the tale from a young man in South Carolina while on vacation. I moved the location to the Suwannee River and the community of Deep Creek, a few miles north of Five Points. The wooden bridge was used until circa 1961 when a logging truck fell through the rotting timbers, killing the father of one of my classmates. A few years later, the bridge mysteriously burnt down. The pilings are still in the river. The idea for "Wallpaper" came from a nightmare I once had.

Keith, Joe Rea and Randy are real people and remain good friends. Jimmy passed in 1993 from the effects of Agent Orange exposure in Vietnam.

ABOUT THE ILLUSTRATOR

Paul N. Massing graduated from Albright Art School in Buffalo, New York, where he studied art and illustrations. Eventually he became an active member of various art organizations in western New York where he had numerous one-man shows and art exhibits. His work is represented in private, corporate and educational institutions in the United States and Canada.

In 1994, Paul found Amelia Island, Florida, to be an inspiring and beautiful setting for his work, so he stayed. He exhibits his work at the Island Art Association in Fernandina Beach, Florida; the St. Augustine Art Association in St. Augustine, Florida; and the Arts Center in St. Petersburg, Florida.

You may contact Paul at paulmassing1@bellsouth.net.

ABOUT THE AUTHOR

Ron Miller grew up in Lake City, Florida, not far from the fabled Suwannee River. There, in the valley of the Suwannee he explored with his friends, the pine forest and gum swamps and fished the plentiful lakes and streams for catfish and brim.

When he had children of his own Ron amused them with tales of his many adventures. That is what inspired him to write it all down. Today he lives on Amelia Island, Florida, with his wife Linda. Together they enjoy a "Brady bunch" family of nine children and eighteen grandchildren.

You may contact Ron at rgmiller59@comcast.net.